THE

HUGUENOTS OF FRANCE;

OR,

THE TIMES OF HENRY IV.

BY THE AUTHOR OF ILVERTON RECTORY, ALLAN CAMERON, EVELYN PERCIVAL, ETC.

PUBLISHED BY THE
AMERICAN TRACT SOCIETY,
150 NASSAU-STREET, NEW YORK.

CONTENTS.

THE HUGUENOTS OF FRANCE; OR THE TIMES OF HENRY FOURTH.

CHAPTER I.

LOOKING BACK.

You have often asked it of me, my good and dutiful children, that I should recall some of the passages of my long and eventful career, in such a manner as to give them permanence as family records. Hitherto I have shrunk from the task,

> "For sorrow's memory is a sorrow still;"

and there were many things connected with the past so painful, that I could not choose voluntarily to recall them.

But time has brought healing on its wings; most of my contemporaries are dead, and to-day the past comes back to me so vividly, that I cannot turn away from it. Once more the silent and deserted halls of memory are filled with fair women and brave men, and the old blood rushes through my veins with something of the fire of youth. I will take advantage of this unwonted mood, to bring back some of those scenes of long ago which attracted the attention of all Europe at the time, and whose effects are yet felt, though more than half a century has passed away.

My own history derives its interest from being closely connected with that of the illustrious prince who forms the central figure in my historic tableau.

My father, the Sieur de Beauvilliers, belonged to an ancient and distinguished family of Navarre, from whom he inherited the estate and chateau of St. Florent, situated near the ancient town of Pau, on a little tributary of the Adour. We were surrounded by mountains, having the wild Cevennes stretching far away on our right, and on the other side the Pyrenees, dimly visible in the distance, forming the southern boundary of French Navarre.

In his early youth my father spent several years in Geneva, and there became acquainted with Calvin, Beza, and other celebrated reformers, from whom he learned the doctrines of the new faith; and before attaining his majority adopted the Protestant belief, to which he continued through life a firm adherent. My mother was descended from a branch of the family of Chatillon, and was related to Admiral Coligny and his brother D'Andelot, the two celebrated leaders of the Huguenots in the early period of their long struggle for religious and civil liberty.

That devotion to the cause of Protestantism which in my father was the result of a passionate love of freedom, rather than of deep religious feeling, was in my gentle mother a matter of fervent conviction; and while her intellect adopted the tenets of the Reformation as undeniable truths, her heart received them into its deepest recesses as the thirsty earth drinks in the blessed dew of heaven. On her lips was the law of kindness, and the most perfect exemplification of Christian character I ever saw or expect to see on earth, was before my eyes from infancy, in the person of that lovely and beloved parent. One sister shared with me the love and tenderness which made our childhood so happy; a bright, joyous girl, with a sensitive nature, which responded like the wind-harp to every breath of joy or sorrow. In those early days our mother was our only instructress, and the hours spent by Aimée and myself in her pleasant dressing-room, learning our daily tasks, while she worked, or wrote, or read beside us, are among the most delightful of my childish recollections.

When lessons were over for the day, we were permitted to wander at will in the vicinity of the chateau, under the care of Claudine, our faithful *bonne*, who loved us so dearly that, to gratify our lightest wish, she would willingly endure any amount of privation and fatigue. We climbed the neighboring mountains, visited the caves and waterfalls hid in their wildest recesses, and made friends of the shepherds who tended their flocks on the upland or in the valley, by the pleasure with which we listened to their simple ballads, and by our interest in the welfare of their fleecy charge. In this way we became hardy and adventurous; so that when I was ten and Aimée eight, few children, even in the mountainous districts of Bearn and Navarre, could excel us in speed or daring. It is certain, however, that Aimée's courage was principally derived from her unselfish affection for her reckless brother. Where I went, she wished always to accompany me, and in her anxiety for my safety, seemed utterly forgetful of her own. My sweet sister, I count it one of the greatest blessings of my lot that, before being exposed to the seductions of the most profligate court of Europe, such models of female purity and excellence had been before me, that I could never doubt the reality of virtue, even in the midst of the most hideous forms of vice. Happy the son and brother who, when vanity and folly are knocking at the door of his young heart, can bid them begone in the sacred name of the mother and sisters whose cherished images already fill the shrine. But alas for his safety if these household memories are only a vanishing dream, destitute alike of tenderness and reality. Among my early friends many belonged to this latter class, and I know that, in their estimation, female virtue was but a marketable commodity, and female truth a myth, which no man in his senses would ever dream of believing.

CHAPTER II.

THE PROTESTANT PASTOR.

ONE afternoon in summer, just before my tenth birthday, Aimée and myself had gone with Claudine to a *chaumiere* or hut among the hills, for the purpose of carrying something from my mother to the sick and poor peasant who occupied it. Our road was full of beauty: now leading through a ravine by the side of a rushing mountain torrent, over which we passed on a rude bridge thrown across by the peasantry; at another time winding through some sheltered forest glade, where the tall trees arching over our heads, and the wild flowers blooming beneath our feet, drew from us exclamations of pleasure at every step.

We had reached a small opening in

the forest covered with verdure, and known to the country people by the name of "The Lady's Bower," from some ancient tradition, when we saw a man of venerable appearance, with hair and beard of snowy whiteness, leaning as he walked on a trusty staff, while a wallet slung over his shoulder marked him as a traveller. He approached as we came in sight, and with a manner peculiarly gentle, inquired if we could tell him the way to the Castle of St. Florent. Claudine was some steps behind us, and I was hesitating what answer to return, when, contrary to her usual custom, for she was timid as a fawn in the presence of strangers, Aimée exclaimed,

"Oh yes, we can, for that is our home, and papa and mamma are there."

"Are you then the daughter of the Sieur de Beauvilliers, my little maiden?" the stranger asked with a pleasant smile.

"Yes, I am his little Aimée, and this is my big brother Henri, who is very brave, and always takes care of me."

"A good character you give him, my little friend, and I trust he may continue to deserve it. But if you are going to the chateau, will you permit me to accompany you, for I was on my way there from Montauban when I lost myself on the mountain."

Without speaking, Aimée placed her little hand confidingly in that of the stranger, and I led the way, while Claudine followed in the rear of the little party.

When we arrived at the chateau, and saw the respect and affection with which our companion was received by our parents, we congratulated ourselves on having brought home a guest so welcome; and our joy was increased on learning that our visitor was the excellent Victor

Fauchet, one of those devoted pastors who in the darkest days of persecution refused to forsake their flock, but went from place to place in constant jeopardy of life, strengthening the weak and comforting the desponding.

This was my first introduction to M. Fauchet, a man to whom I afterwards owed so much, and my childish heart was drawn to him at once, for there was in his aspect a sweetness mingled with dignity which was singularly attractive. I was never happier than when attending him in the long walks he was accustomed to take among the hills in search of the scattered members of his flock.

None but those who have belonged to a proscribed and persecuted church can imagine the joy with which those hunted disciples, hiding in dens and caves, greeted a spiritual guide so loved and trusted as M. Fauchet. They welcomed him with tears of joy; they hung on his words with breathless interest; and when he left them, thanked God that they had once more enjoyed the privilege of looking in his face, and prayed for a thousand blessings on his head. The good pastor had not been long at St. Florent, when my father proposed to him to take charge of my education, which until then had been carried on in a very desultory manner. As Henry II. of France, urged on by the Cardinal Lorraine, was doing all in his power to destroy the Huguenots, M. Fauchet accepted the proposition, on the condition that when a wider field of usefulness might open, he should be at liberty to leave.

My father was often absent from home, being entrusted by his sovereign, the aged king of Navarre, with various important missions to the court of France, the Low Countries, and England, whose lion-hearted queen was looked upon as the hope and stay of Protestantism throughout Europe.

On one of these occasions, when M. Fauchet and I had been absent for some hours, on our return we found the chateau in a state of unusual commotion. The courtyard was filled with men and horses, and as soon as my companion saw the badges worn by the former, with an exclamation of surprise he hastened into the house. Lights were gleaming in every apartment, servants were carrying and obeying orders, and it was some time before I could find my mother or sister to inquire what had happened to turn our quiet abode into such a scene of confusion.

"Why, Henri," said Aimée with a little air of importance, "do n't you know our mother has a cousin who is a brave soldier and such a great man, and his name is D'Andelot, and he came here to-day with papa, and they are in the saloon?"

"Papa here, and I knew nothing of it!" I exclaimed as I ran into the saloon to see and welcome him. My father introduced me to the famous Huguenot leader, who received me with marked kindness, saying to my father,

"Your boy, my good lord, is a genuine scion of the old Norman stock, and will, I am sure, do honor to the name. As for my fair cousin here, she has transmitted the traits of her southern blood to this little blossom," pointing to Aimée, who was in her usual place of refuge, the arms of my good tutor.

General D'Andelot gave to my father and M. Fauchet the particulars of an interview between the king of France and himself; and though I was thought to be too young to take an interest in the conversation, the incident made an indelible impression on my mind. The two brothers, Coligny and D'Andelot, had both embraced the reformed religion; but the admiral, naturally calm and reserved, said little about his new faith, though he would have died for it cheerfully, while D'Andelot boldly avowed his principles on all occasions, and denounced the church of Rome as antichrist. Henry, whose first lessons in war were taken from the famous general, refused to believe him a heretic, and would hear nothing against the stout old warrior, until he was induced by Cardinal Lorraine to summon the accused to Paris to answer for himself.

At the table of his royal master the brave Huguenot not only avowed his firm belief in the doctrines of the Reformation, but declared that he regarded the popish sacrifice of the mass as an act of gross impiety. The monarch was both bigoted and irritable; and this confession excited his wrath to such a degree, that he started from the table, and seizing a plate, was about to hurl it at the man who had ventured thus to brave his anger. He held it poised for a moment; then, like a child who dares not give full vent to his wrath, he threw it to the floor with such violence that one of the fragments wounded the dauphin, afterwards Francis II., who was sitting by him at the table. D'Andelot retired from the presence of the king, but was arrested the same day and thrown into prison, where he remained for some months, until released through the influence of his uncle the Constable Montmorenci, while the church of Rome was urging the French king to have him burned as a heretic. The hero sternly refused to renounce, or even to conceal his faith:

still the offices of which he had been deprived were restored to him one by one, and the Protestant cause seemed to have gained a triumph in the successful resistance of a man so renowned to the power of the Pope.

While he remained at the chateau it was a scene of constant bustle and excitement. Messengers were coming and going from different quarters, the neighboring gentry who were friends to the Huguenot cause came together frequently, and every thing indicated the presence of a master-spirit in the province. My father entered heart and soul into the plans of the general; but my mother, clasping Aimée in her arms, prayed fervently that the bloody strife, which she plainly foresaw, might, if possible, still be averted.

"We have always prospered most as a church," she said to my father, "when most obscure and depressed. I fear, my dear lord, lest in the heat of civil strife the pure precepts of our divine Master may be forgotten or disregarded."

"Thou art so nearly a saint, sweet wife," he replied, "that I almost fear to see thee unfold some hidden wings and float upward before mine eyes. But I and my brethren in arms, while we are in the flesh, must have some regard to the saving of our bodies as well as souls, and I warrant thee that to do this something besides prayer is necessary."

"It may be so; but do not forget, dear husband and lord, that a religion of externals only is not worth fighting for, and only while we maintain the life of God in our hearts can we expect his blessing on our efforts even in his service."

CHAPTER III.

JANE D'ALBRET AND HENRY OF NAVARRE.

SOON after the departure of the Huguenot chief, my father was summoned on business to the castle of Pau, at that time the residence of the court of Navarre, and for the first time in my life I was permitted to accompany him. The castle was a grand and imposing structure, built on a bold eminence on the Gave, a small, sluggish stream which, after winding its way between low-lying banks through most of its course, falls at length into the Garonne.

The numerous tapering and concave roofs of this old kingly residence, its salient angles, its towers and curtains, embrasures and loops, give it an appearance of great antiquity as well as strength, and render it venerable and grand, rather than picturesque, in its general appearance. Like most feudal castles, it is built round a wide courtyard in the centre, from whence you look up to irregular ranges of windows and carved masonry, even then worn and grey with time. The state apartments overlooked the river and valley, and just below them is a broad terrace on which a garden had been planted, with straight rows of plum and pear trees running through it at right angles.

My father entered the chateau through the grand portal situated between two frowning and impregnable towers, and was ushered at once into the cabinet of the king, leaving me alone in the antechamber. I was examining the objects around me with childish curiosity, when a page touched my arm, and bidding me follow him, led the way into the garden of which I have spoken. I followed my guide up one alley and down another, until we came to a place where several persons were standing, among whom my boyish instinct at once selected the Duchess de Vendome, only child of the king of Navarre, and heiress to the throne. Her dress was simple, even to severity, and she wore no insignia of rank, but there was an innate dignity in her air and manner which could not be mistaken. Without hesitation I approached her, and kneeling, kissed the hand she extended to me, as I had been taught was the etiquette on such occasions. The duchess smiled graciously, and said to one of her attendants,

"See, Justine, the varlet knows where his homage is due. It would be well if his elders had equal sagacity."

The young lady blushed at this remark, which she seemed to understand, and turning away, left me with the princess, who questioned me concerning my parents, sister, and myself, to which I returned answers as brief as possible, for I was far from feeling at ease in my present situation. Jane D'Albret, afterwards Queen of Navarre, and one of the nursing-mothers of the Reformation in France, was a tall and finely formed woman, with a carriage full of grace and dignity, and an eye that pierced one like a flash of light. Her face was grave and almost stern when in repose, but her smile had a marvellous sweetness, and her voice was low and musical in its tones. She was more highly educated than most women of rank of that day, and understood thoroughly all the arts of diplomacy, though she loathed the vile intrigues in which her political rival Catharine de Medicis was constantly engaged.

But it is not to be supposed that all this was before my mind as I stood beside the princess in the garden. On the contrary, my attention was absorbed in watching the movements of a boy apparently of my own age, who was coming slowly towards us, in obedience to the summons of a page.

"Come hither, my son," said the duchess, holding out her hand to the boy, "and let me present to you a playfellow, and I hope a future friend, in Henri de Beauvilliers, the son of our dear and well-tried friends at St. Florent."

The boy kissed his mother's hand with the easy grace of a much older courtier, and then turning to me, said with a frank courtesy which well became his open and joyous countenance,

"I am glad to see a namesake who looks as if he would not disgrace the name. There are three Henries of us already: Henry of Anjou, Henry of Guise, and Henry of Navarre; and now there is a fourth, Henri de Beauvilliers."

He laughed with boyish glee as he said this, and I joined heartily in the merriment, after which we soon found ourselves on terms of tolerable intimacy. He took me to see his splendid Spanish jennet, his falcons, and a mimic fortification of his own construction, and said to me confidentially,

"I don't live here, you must know, for my grandfather thinks a prince should never be trained up by women; so I live at the Castle of Courasse with my tutor M. Montfauçon, and I assure you that the poorest peasant-boy in Bearn does not sleep or fare more hardly than his prince. But I care not, for it will all make me more brave and bold, and my motto is, 'Conquer or die.' I mean to do it too, when I am old enough," he continued, his fine face all in a glow, "for I have just been to the Court of France with my parents, and though I am only a boy, I could read that wicked queen as easy as my missal. She hates my mother and me, and would hate my father, only that she is not afraid of him. But never mind; I shall be a man some day, and then they shall fear, if they do not love me, or I am much mistaken."

I looked on my young companion with a feeling of awe as he uttered these words in a tone of stern determination so unsuited to his years. A few moments since he was a laughing, happy boy; now he stood there with all a man's firmness and decision written on his brow. Nature had evidently formed him for command, and he seemed to me then, what I always afterwards considered him, the very model of a princely leader of brave men.

Such was my first interview with Henry of Navarre, afterwards the celebrated Henry Fourth of France—Henri Quatre; and from that hour to the day of his early and lamented death, I loved him as a brother, and revered him as one of the noblest and bravest of men.

In a few weeks after my visit to Pau, the old king died, and Anthony Duc de Vendome and his wife Jane D'Albret succeeded him as king and queen of Navarre. They went to Paris soon after the accession, with the young prince, to be present at the marriage of the Dauphin Francis to Mary Stuart the beautiful and unfortunate queen of Scotland. Henry of Navarre was even then greatly admired for his manly and engaging qualities; and it was remarked of him by an old courtier, that he was more of a king in person and manners than his father, or his cousin the king of France.

After the return of the king and queen to Navarre, the education of the young prince went on as usual, though he now resided with the court at Pau or Nerae, where the royal family spent several months of every year. He came often to St. Florent, and as my holidays were usually spent with him, we became inseparable. Aimée sometimes complained that she had lost her brother; for as we grew older, our tastes and amusements became more dissimilar, and when the young prince was with me, our sports were of a nature so daring, and as they now seem to me so foolhardy, that it was quite impossible for Aimée to join us. Still I almost worshipped my gentle and beautiful sister, and was never happier than when I could persuade the prince to join me in preparing for her some little surprise on a festival or birthday. Henry was inclined to look down on the gentler sex from the height of a fancied superiority, and looked upon it as a condescension on our part to seek to give pleasure to a young girl. But he was too good-natured to refuse, and the innocent delight manifested by Aimée when she found us planning for her enjoyment, was a sufficient reward for all our toil.

CHAPTER IV.

CLOUDS IN THE POLITICAL HORIZON.

WHILE in the quiet province of Navarre we were amusing ourselves with the sports and recreations of youth, the most important changes were going on in other portions of the kingdom, of which we as yet knew nothing.

Henry II. was dead, having been killed in a mock tournament by a splinter from the lance of his antagonist passing through his eye into the brain. Francis II., the husband of Mary Stuart, was nominally king, though the queen mother Catharine de Medicis was in reality at the head of affairs.

The kingdom was agitated to its centre by religious dissensions, and as a last resort, a conference was proposed between some of the leading reformers on one side, and the Cardinal Lorraine on the other, in which all points of difference should be fully and freely discussed. All the great dignitaries of the kingdom were invited to be present, and though at first the plan was opposed by the Pope, he yielded at length, and the disputants met at a place called Poissy, whence the conference was called the "Colloquy of Poissy."

Theodore Beza, Peter Martyr, and others less distinguished, were present, and for several days pleaded the cause of the Reformation with so much learning, moderation, and piety, that Queen Jane of Navarre, who was present, became a convert to the truth, which was ever after dearer to her than life. Her husband, on the other hand, weak and vacillating, though he had previously favored the new doctrines, went back to Romanism, frightened, as he said, to see the wide difference between the two systems, which he had supposed very nearly connected. The young prince, however, was committed to the care of his mother, to be trained up in her faith, as Anthony was unwilling to burden himself with the care of his education.

When the conference was ended the queen returned to Navarre, but the king remained in Paris, vainly hoping to obtain from the court a recognition of his rights as the first Peer of France and Governor of Guienne. This was denied; and instead of solid advantages, the doubtful distinction was accorded him of escorting the young Princess Elizabeth, who had been recently betrothed to the king of Spain, to Bayonne, where her husband was to receive his bride. The royal party passed through Navarre, and spent a few days at Nerac, where all was life and gayety during their stay. The young queen of Spain was charmed with her boy cousin, and the attachment then formed, strengthened as it was by a subsequent interview, was the means of saving Henry and his mother from the dungeons of the Inquisition. A plot had been formed by the king of Spain, the Pope, and Catharine de Medicis, to seize Queen Jane and her son, and convey them over the Pyrenees into Spain, when the inquisitor-general was to relieve them of all further care in the disposal of the illustrious victims. Just before this nefarious plan was to have been carried out, it came to the knowledge of the queen through one of her gentlemen in waiting, to whom the chief agent had confessed it while dangerously sick in Madrid. Elizabeth sent instant warning to the queen of Navarre, who took measures to provide for her own safety and that of her son. She also despatched a messenger to Paris, to inform the queen mother of the base treachery contemplated by Philip and the Pope. Catharine, hoping that her share in the project was not suspected, instantly gave orders for the arrest of the agents, who were sacrificed to secure the safety of their perfidious mistress.

Meanwhile the young Henry, the object of so many hopes and fears, plots and counterplots throughout the kingdom, was quietly pursuing a course of mental and physical training at the college of Montauban. The four Henries—Henry of Anjou, afterwards Henry III. of France; Henry of Guise, the bloody leader of St. Bartholomew; Henry of Navarre, and Henri de Beauvilliers—were all members of one class, and inseparable companions. The prince of Bearn and myself were stouter and better grown than the others, and I may say without vanity that we were far in advance of them in intellectual attainments, since in my own case it was all owing, under God, to my excellent tutor and friend M. Fauchet.

It has been said there is no royal road to learning; but of him it was certainly true, that he knew how to make the path of knowledge so attractive, that it was a pleasure to walk therein.

Henry of Anjou was vain, frivolous, and crafty, devoted to low pleasures, and incapable of generous emotions. Henry of Guise, at that period of his life, seemed honest and constant in his attachment to his friends, but haughty, revengeful, and implacable to his enemies. My prince was then what he continued through life, frank, generous, and forbearing almost to a fault, brave and chivalric as the Spanish Cid, but so fond of pleasure and amusement as sometimes to sacrifice the most important interests in their pursuit. But even while one blamed, it was impossible to avoid loving him; and never, since the days of Edward the Black Prince of England, had there been a leader more fitted in every way to awaken the enthusiastic devotion of his followers than Henry of Navarre.

I was fifteen, and the prince a few months older, when we were summoned to Nerae, where the court then was, to meet the queen mother, who was on a progress through the kingdom, intending to visit her daughter the queen of Spain. She was accompanied by a bevy of beautiful young maidens, among whom her daughter Margaret of Valois, a girl of fourteen, shone conspicuous for grace and beauty. In conformity with her crafty plan of flattering the Huguenots, the more effectually to destroy them,

Catharine made a long stay at Nerae, where she exerted her utmost skill in captivating the imagination of the young prince, in whom the crafty Italian already saw a powerful ally, or a dangerous enemy. She called him her son, and spoke openly of the wish of the two kings of France and Navarre for a union between Henry and Margaret. She threw the young people constantly together; but Margaret, who was at that early age a finished coquette, had taken a decided aversion to her cousin, and on his part he was totally indifferent to her charms. Absorbed as he was in higher pursuits, there were no symptoms at that age of the fatal subjection to female charms which exerted so unhappy an influence over him in after-life.

When Catharine left Nerae, the queen of Navarre, with a brilliant retinue, among whom was my sweet sister Aimée, accompanied her to Bayonne, where we were met by the queen of Spain, with a numerous escort of Spanish grandees. Among all this assembly, made up of the flower of the French and Spanish courts, Henry of Navarre was first in all manly graces and acquirements, insomuch that the Duke of Medina exclaimed,

"It seems to me that this young prince is either an emperor in disguise, or deserves to be one."

Nature had made him every inch a king, and the teachings of his mother were well calculated to develop the resources of a singularly ardent and gifted mind. She kept constantly before him the fact that he had been solemnly dedicated to the defence of the Protestant faith; and the year following the visit to Spain, when war was again raging between the Catholics and Huguenots, she brought Henry to the camp at Tonnay

Charente, where the forces were assembled, and in an animated address pointed him out to the troops as the destined leader of the Protestant cause.

"My son is still young," she said; "but I, who have read him like an open book from infancy, tell you that if his life is spared, you will know that God has raised him up for this special purpose, endowing him with the very qualities necessary for it. Meantime you have in Admiral Coligny a general who, from his wisdom, skill, and valor, ranks among the foremost captains of Europe."

The army received its young chief with the greatest enthusiasm, and could hardly be persuaded to suffer him to return to Navarre for the completion of his education. His father was killed soon after this at the siege of Rouen, and it became necessary for Jane and her son to visit the French court. They were cordially received and treated with great kindness; but when the queen left Paris, Henry was detained on some trifling pretence, and for more than a year remained in a kind of honorable captivity in Paris. To the repeated messages of Jane, answers were returned which convinced her that Catharine did not intend to suffer him to leave for Navarre. With her usual courage and decision, the queen went instantly to Paris, and after a week of waiting, during which her plans were formed, she succeeded in escaping with her son during a grand hunt in the forest of Fontainebleau. A few faithful followers were in waiting, and the little party travelled day and night until they reached a place of safety. The queen mother was excessively indignant, but with her usual skill at dissembling, she sent friendly messages to

Queen Jane, assuring her that Henry had always been at liberty to depart, and that she desired nothing more fervently than a union between the two houses, which should insure the tranquillity of France.

CHAPTER V.

ADELE DE BRIANCOURT.

After my return from the camp, whither I accompanied the queen and prince, I went back to Montauban to resume the course of study interrupted by that event. Of all the four Henries, only one besides myself, the young duke of Guise, remained; and as we had never suited each other, I was quite alone. M. Fauchet came often to Montauban to visit a grandchild who was at school there, but I had never seen her, and was ignorant even of her name.

One summer evening—how well I remember the time!—when there had been a festival of some kind in the town, and the streets were unusually full of noise and riot, I was returning from college to my lodgings, when I saw before me two females walking hastily and evidently anxious to avoid observation. They were muffled in heavy cloaks, which nearly concealed the face and form, but enough of both was visible to show that one of them was young and beautiful. They had nearly reached the public square, when in a narrow alley leading to it they were rudely assailed by two ruffians, who attempted to pull the cloak away from the younger of the two, exclaiming with an oath that they had found a prize, and would not let it go. Not a word was spoken by the lady, though she struggled bravely to release herself from the grasp of the villain, but the other female uttered shriek upon shriek as she saw her companion in such peril. Without waiting to think of the odds against me, I drew the short sword worn by young noblemen at that time, and rushing forward, gave a sudden thrust at the taller of the two fellows, which compelled him to relinquish his hold. It was so dark that he could not at once distinguish his assailant, and as a crowd was collecting, called together by the screams of the woman, both the men fled; and though pursued by one or two officers, succeeded in making their escape. Meantime the young lady turned to me, and in a voice which seemed to me the most musical I had ever heard, thanked me for my timely assistance, and requested me to make way for them through the crowd, as they wished to escape as quickly as possible. Having done this, and escorted them in safety to the public square, the unknown turned to me, saying,

"We are near home and in perfect security; here then we must part, but accept our thanks for your great kindness, and be assured we shall never forget it."

"No thanks are due to me," I replied, "for a common act of humanity. I should be a degenerate Beauvilliers if I could be deaf to the call of insulted womanhood."

"Beauvilliers!" she repeated; "can this be Henri Beauvilliers of St. Florent?"

"It certainly is the same; but how am I so happy as to be known to you?"

"Oh, that is easily explained," she replied with the charming frankness which marked her character; "I am Adele Briancourt, the grandchild of your tutor M. Fauchet, and he has talked of you so much that I seem to know you well. How strange that you should be the one to save me from those fearful men;" and she shuddered as she spoke. The voice was music, the language indicated culture and refinement, but the face—ah, that was concealed by the envious darkness that shrouded us in its mantle.

"And now that you know who I am, dear lady, will you not allow me to accompany you home?"

"Not to-night," she replied quickly, "for I wish to get in as quietly as possible; but at any other time, if you choose to call on Madame Toulan my aunt, she will doubtless be glad to welcome you, and I should be very ungrateful to be otherwise."

I was obliged to content myself with this admission, but as I retraced my steps towards home my thoughts were occupied with the adventure, and I resolved to follow out the acquaintance as speedily as possible. Two days afterwards I called at the house of Madame Toulan, and was formally introduced to her niece

Mademoiselle Briancourt. She was two years younger than I, but far more mature in person and mind, though she had all the simplicity and joyous freshness of early youth. Her large hazel eyes were soft and pleading as those of the gazelle, though when flashing with deep emotion they were brilliant as stars; and in that sweetest face one might read, as in a mirror, every feeling of the soul. She was taller than Aimée and more critically beautiful, but the same dove-like innocence and purity beamed through every expressive feature of both these fair maidens.

Adele, as an orphan, had been early thrown on her own resources, while Aimée, tenderly sheltered and cherished, was strong only through her affections. To my great surprise no allusion was made by Adele to the adventure of the Rue de Marais, and in the presence of her aunt she received me as a stranger. But when Madame Toulan was called from the room, her manner changed instantly as she said with a smile,

"I must waive ceremony, monsieur, while I explain to you in a few words the situation in which you found me the other night. It was absolutely necessary to get word to my grandfather and M. Beauvilliers of a plot formed by the Duke of Guise to gain possession of the young prince and carry him to Paris. There was no one but myself to act as messenger, since my aunt, though good and true, is unfortunately fond of talking, and cannot keep a secret. I was obliged therefore to take a faithful servant, and go by stealth to find the young lad who carries letters from here to St. Florent, and from thence to Montauban. We were unavoidably delayed and you know the rest."

"But was your errand successful?" I inquired, for I had a deep interest in the result.

"I trust so, as the lad was found at last and instantly sent off to the chateau We have so many secret friends scattered over the country, that it is nearly impossible for our enemies to keep their designs wholly concealed from us. But more than all, God is on our side, and you know he can make one to chase a thousand, and two to put ten thousand to flight."

The face of the young enthusiast was radiant with faith and hope, and in my admiration I had unconsciously drawn nearer to her than our supposed acquaintance warranted; so as a step was heard approaching, I resumed my seat, and with it the formality which became me as a stranger. My endeavor to please madame was so far successful, that she gave me a cordial invitation to renew my visit, a compliment which I need not say was thankfully accepted.

I went again and again, and usually saw Adele on these occasions, though once or twice I fancied, from the arch look on her sunny face, that she was not sorry to plead an engagement, which left me alone to play the agreeable to her aunt, a task so adroitly performed, that the good lady averred she had never met a young gentleman of so much good sense and judgment as M. Henri Beauvilliers.

Her house, from which until now all young men, and especially members of the college, had been rigidly excluded, was always open to me, and for the first time since going to Montauban, I found the town so pleasant a place of residence, that the thought of change was unwelcome.

CHAPTER VI.

HOURS OF SUNSHINE.

If my vanity was ever fed by the good opinion of Madame Toulan, it experienced a salutary drawback in the very different manner of her young companion. One day when I had been so foolish as to address Adele in the strain of flattery and compliment in vogue at the French court, she turned to me suddenly, saying,

"Henri, my friend, you are doing strange injustice to yourself and me. You are attempting to pass off false coin upon me for true. It is counterfeit, and you know it, so it is utterly worthless in my eyes. If we were both older, I should think it necessary to be indignant; but as we are little more than children, I tell you plainly I like you far better as your own honest self, than when you borrow French frippery and folly."

I felt very much like the traveller in the fairy tale, who, on bringing forward his beads and trinkets to propitiate the favor of the inhabitants of a certain city, found them all transformed into rags and pebble-stones. Adele saw my mortification, and laughed gayly.

"You need not look so disconcerted, Henri; for if I cannot appreciate insincere compliments, I can understand kind deeds and noble sentiments, and these, I am sure, I may always expect from a Beauvilliers."

How sweet were the hours spent in the society of this lovely and innocent maiden, whose thoughts and feelings had all the dewy freshness of life's early morn, combined with the maturity of riper years. Hitherto I had known the other sex chiefly through my mother and sister, who were to me types of all that is lovely or estimable in woman. During my short stay at the French court, I was shocked at the forwardness and disgusted with the frivolity of the beauties who fluttered about the queen mother, and boy as I was, turned away with a sick heart from all their fascinations. But here was a young girl who possessed beauty without vanity, wit without bitterness, and a power of attraction I had never seen equalled, without the slightest taint of coquetry. Still no thought of love came to trouble my dream of happiness. Adele was to me only an older and more charming Aimée; and if we had been in reality children of the same parents, our intercourse could not have been more strictly fraternal in its character.

In France, at that day, parents had

the absolute disposal of their children in marriage, and no consideration of mutual affection was ever suffered to influence them in forming the nuptial contract. This state of things prevented a healthful development of the affections even in those rare instances in which any thing like intimacy existed between the sexes. The higher nobility, it is true, cared little for the laws of God or man on this subject, but the influence of our good queen had thus far preserved Bearn and Navarre from the moral contagion which overspread the other provinces of France. Our young prince had been so long at the court of Catharine, that his principles were in some degree unsettled, and his manners had not wholly escaped the infection; but the standard of morality among both classes, the lords and peasantry, was far higher in the remote provinces than elsewhere.

Adele de Briancourt was the daughter of a Flemish nobleman who married the only child of M. Fauchet, taking her to Bruges, whither her father soon followed. M. Briancourt had been appointed by William of Orange governor of the important town and fortress of Courtrai, which place he gallantly defended for weeks against a large body of Spanish troops sent by Philip of Spain to reduce it. In a sortie made by the garrison, with the hope of compelling the enemy to raise the siege, the brave governor lost his life; and as no reinforcements were sent from William, Courtrai was forced to surrender, making the best terms possible with a savage and infuriated foe. The town was given up to sack and pillage; but by a providence almost miraculous, M. Fauchet, with his widowed daughter and her infant child, escaped over the frontier, and made their way to Montauban, as M. Briancourt had a sister residing in that town.

The fugitives were kindly received and sheltered by Madame Toulan, who was a widow in easy circumstances, and strongly attached to the Protestant faith, though her propensity to gossip made her an unsafe depositary of state secrets. After seeing his daughter comfortably settled, M. Fauchet resumed his former employment, that of visiting churches and individuals of the reformed faith, who were scattered throughout France. The father and child never met again. Before his return the youthful widow had gone where the wicked cease from troubling, and the weary are at rest, leaving the young Adele to the care of her grandfather and aunt, by both of whom she was cherished as the most precious thing on earth. Her education had been carefully conducted, and though she lived in strict retirement, the native refinement and grace of her manners fitted her for any society in the land.

On my first visit at St. Florent after meeting Adele, I related the circumstances to my mother and sister, begging the former to invite her to the chateau, as Aimée had never enjoyed the pleasure of companionship with a young girl of her own age and rank. As I closed my earnest appeal, my dear mother replied with a smile,

"You are a skilful pleader, my Henri; but even if I were to consent to your suit, which I am strongly inclined to do, you forget that there is another to be consulted, who might regard the subject in quite another light. From the fact that our friend M. Fauchet has never spoken to us of bringing his grandchild hither, I imagine you would have some difficulty in gaining his consent to the proposal."

"Have I your permission to make the attempt now, my mother?"

"You have it, my son, and my very best wishes for your success, for I see in my Aimée's eyes that she is longing for a sight of this promised friend and companion."

The pastor was absent with my father, but I took the first opportunity after his return of addressing him on the subject. He heard me patiently, and answered with his usual kindness,

"I have not been ignorant, my young friend, of the acquaintance between you and my grandchild, for every thing that concerns her is important to me. But for my perfect confidence in you both, the intercourse would long since have been broken up, for there can be nothing in common between you and her. Nay, my son, you need not exonerate yourself. I know full well that no thoughts but those of friendship have entered your heart; but I have long studied human nature, and I know too that friendship between two young persons like yourself and Adele, neither of whom are destitute of attractions, is not exactly safe for either. But you have nearly reached manhood, and stirring times are coming—times which demand the best energies of all who love the Protestant cause to save our threatened liberties. Your father is about to join Condé, who is in arms, and will take you with him, that your first lessons in war may be taken under his eye and at his side. Then, if your mother wishes for the society of my child to enliven the solitude of your sister, it will be my duty and pleasure to bring her to the chateau."

I was far from being satisfied with this concession; but the joy with which I found that I was to join my father at the camp of Condé overcame every other feeling. In a few weeks I took leave of Montauban and of Adele, who said to me with glowing cheeks and sparkling eyes, as she gave me her hand,

"You are going, my friend, to fight for that which is dearer to us both than life itself; but do not forget that you leave a mother and two sisters, to whom your safety is very precious, and who will be constantly praying for your welfare and success."

I could only utter the word farewell; but as I turned away the secret vow was registered in heaven, that with God's help I would prove myself worthy the affection lavished on me by those beloved ones who were watching and praying for me at home.

I cannot go into the particulars of my first campaign. Marchings and counter-marchings, successes and defeats, all are mingled together in my remembrance of those months in camp. The glorious banner of Condé, on which was inscribed, "It is sweet to brave danger for Christ and our country," was on one occasion near falling into the hands of the enemy. The standard-bearer was down, pierced with innumerable wounds; but still, with hands stiffening in death, clinging to the broken staff, when it was my good fortune to rescue and carry back the banner in safety. For this I received the thanks of the great leader, and as one of his aids was selected to be the bearer of despatches to the queen of Navarre.

I spent a few delightful hours at St. Florent with my mother, sister, and Adele. How little I imagined they were the last peaceful ones I was ever to know in that endeared spot. But I will not anticipate.

Finding it impossible to overcome

Condé in open warfare, Catharine contrived, by means of false pretences and protestations, to draw the hero to Paris, where he was arrested and thrown into prison. After a mock trial he was sentenced to death, but at the last moment saved from the scaffold by the death of Francis II. After the accession of the next brother, Charles IX., Condé was released, and a treaty signed between the contending parties, which soon shared the fate of those which had gone before.

CHAPTER VII.

THE HUGUENOTS INVITED TO PARIS.

I HAD been in the army nearly two years, when, in the bloody battle of Jarnac, our brave leader the Duke de Condé, was slain. While the troops were forming for battle, he received a kick on the leg from the horse of the Count Rochefoucauld, who was standing near him ready to mount. So terrible was the blow, that the bone instantly protruded through his military boot; but Condé would not leave the field for surgical attendance.

"Behold," he said to those about him, "behold, ye true nobility of France, the moment we have so much desired. Let us go forward to finish what is so well begun, and remember the state in which

Louis of Bourbon enters the field for his country and his Redeemer."

With these words he gave the orders for a charge, and poured his men like a torrent into the midst of the enemy. For a moment all gave way before him; but soon the main body of the French, under Henry of Anjou, with the German mercenaries, surrounded us on all sides. Every man of the Protestants fought with desperate valor, and twenty brave fellows cut their way through every thing, carrying with them the banner of Condé. But that heroic prince had fought his last battle. With his leg fractured in two places, wounded in the arm, and his horse killed under him, he fell to the ground, and was stabbed to the heart by one who recognized the Huguenot leader in that terrible condition. Condé was a brave soldier and a far-seeing statesman, though far from being as single-hearted in his devotion to the cause of religious liberty as the aged Admiral Coligny, who after the death of Condé became the leader of the Huguenot armies.

In the same battle of Jarnac, my father received a wound, which, after a few days of intense suffering, put an end to his life, leaving me the sole protector of my mother and Aimée, and the leader of the Beauvilliers troops, a body of nearly four hundred men. I had little leisure to mourn for him, for dangers surrounded us on every side, and but for a special interposition of Providence, our little army must have been destroyed. But the God who turns the counsels of the wise into foolishness, suffered our foes to fall into discussions among themselves, so that we had time to reorganize our shattered forces, and to push the war with such vigor that Catharine began to tremble for the safety of the capital.

Henry of Navarre, who had reached the years and stature of manhood, and whose every look and word proclaimed him born to command, had joined the army with Count Louis of Navarre, brother of the Prince of Orange, and the Count de Montgomery; and with these illustrious personages were many others of less note, but whose valor had been proved in a hundred well-fought fields. The Protestant array was so threatening, and the success of our enterprises so decided, that the queen mother despaired of subduing the heretics by force of arms, and prevailed upon her son to sign a treaty of peace at St. Germain in August, 1570, to the great joy of the moderate party on both sides. There can be little doubt that the crafty Florentine had even then conceived the infamous project, whose execution, two years later, made all Europe recoil with horror. She was willing therefore to concede nearly all that the Huguenots desired, the better to collect them within the fatal grasp which was to crush them at one blow. A proposal was formally made to Queen Jane, who with her son was in Rochelle during the winter of 1570–71, that a strong and lasting bond of union should be formed between the two parties, by the marriage of the Prince of Navarre to Margaret of Valois, second daughter of Catharine. The proposal, for many reasons, was extremely distasteful to the Queen of Navarre, who distrusted the sincerity of Catharine, and felt that she was most to be feared when most she seemed to smile. But both parties were exhausted with civil war; peace and toleration were blessings inestimable, and reasons of state policy overpowered private feelings, and in an evil hour she consented to the ill-omened union.

As soon as spring should open, the queen was to proceed to Paris, followed by Admiral Coligny and all the principal Huguenot leaders to whom special invitations had been sent by the king and queen mother, and early in the summer Henry was to be in Paris, when the marriage would take place. During the winter, the monotony of camp life was agreeably varied by a double wedding, which took place under rather peculiar circumstances. Jacqueline D'Entremont, a lady of large possessions in Savoy, had become so much interested in the noble character of Admiral Coligny, who was a widower, that through a mutual friend she made him an offer of her heart and hand. The proposal, coming as it did from one whom he knew to be worthy and estimable, was gratefully received by the admiral, who sent a messenger to express his pleasure and gratitude for her favorable opinion. But the Duke of Savoy, who was unwilling that the immense estates of the lady should pass from Savoy into the hands of a heretic, opposed the plan violently, and forbade the marriage. The lady, however, was equally determined with himself; and in such a case the issue is seldom doubtful. She made her escape secretly, and fled to Rochelle, where she was received by the admiral with as much respect and affection as if she had come attended by the whole court of Savoy. In a short time they were married; and at the same time Louise, the daughter of the admiral, gave her hand to her father's tried friend and comrade, the Lord of Teligny.

These double nuptials were celebrated with all the splendor we could command in our narrow quarters, and gave universal satisfaction to the Huguenot party. My mother and sister were in the train of Queen Jane, and I had the pleasure of seeing my sweet Aimée an object of admiration to all who had the privilege of being admitted to her society, not less for the truly feminine delicacy which characterized her, than for her rare and perfect loveliness. On the departure of the queen for Paris, these beloved ones returned to St. Florent, where Adele and her grandfather awaited them.

As I had command of the guards appointed to attend the queen, I took leave of my friends at Rochelle, and the same day started on the journey which was to have so tragic a termination.

CHAPTER VIII.

THE MARRIAGE OF THE PRINCE.

On our arrival in Paris, the queen was received by Catharine with lavish demonstrations of respect, and lodged sumptuously in the Louvre. All was mirth and gayety about the court; but the queen was ill at ease, and regarded the splendid pageantry as only the cover of deep and dark designs, whose scope she was unable to fathom.

One evening, a few weeks after our arrival, as I was about to leave her, after arranging the guards for the night, she called me to her, and laying her hand upon my shoulder, said earnestly,

"My son, you are very dear to me, for your parents' sake as well as for your own, and I tremble for you in this abode of sin and death. I know not why, but my heart is strangely heavy to-night, and misgives me sorely. I fear that we have been entrapped here, I and my people, as silly sheep for the slaughter; and but for the hope of peace, would even now warn the prince not to venture himself in Paris. But God is above all, and to him I commit myself; only remember, Henri Beauvilliers, that Jane of Navarre trusts you as she trusted your noble father, and entreats you to be the same fearless, watchful friend to her impetuous son that the Sieur de Beauvilliers has always been to me."

There was a solemnity in her manner which filled me with a vague alarm.

"You are sad, to-night, dear and honored lady," I said; "permit me to remain within call, that I may watch over your safety while you sleep. Believe me, my royal mistress, this precaution may be necessary."

"Not so, my son," she replied with a smile; "if danger menaces me, it will not come in a form so palpable that human care could meet or avert it. The ruling spirit in this fearful abode knows how to summon earth and air to aid her in securing her revenge. Something seems to tell me that my days are numbered; but I know in whom I have believed, and do not fear to die. I only mourn to leave my son and friends in the trap which has been set for them. But it is late, and your young eyes require sleep. Good-night, my son. May God and all good angels watch over and protect you."

With this solemn blessing she dismissed me, and the next morning, when I returned to the wing of the palace in which the Queen of Navarre and her suite were lodged, I found her so ill as to be insensible to every thing about her. In this state she languished for nine days, and then expired, without one interval of consciousness. I believed then, and believe still, that she died a victim to the hatred of Catharine de Medicis. Her illness was so brief there was no time to send for the prince, who did not arrive until some time after the burial. His grief and indignation were excessive, and his suspicions so strongly aroused, that for a while the deeply laid schemes of the queen mother were in danger of being thwarted by one whom she considered a mere boy. But her pretended sympathy, her flatteries, and cajoling words, together with the representations of Admiral Coligny, whose confidence in Charles and his mother amounted to infatuation, at length overcame his resentment. He yielded, though with evident bitterness of heart, and the preparations for the marriage, which was deferred on account of the death of Queen Jane, went forward.

Margaret of Valois was eighteen, beautiful, witty, and graceful, but so utterly destitute of moral principle, that she scorned to wear even the semblance of propriety. She heartily detested her intended bridegroom, and looked on the court of Navarre as a purgatory, into which she was to be banished, and from which she prayed speedily to be delivered. On the other hand, the young king of Navarre, as he had become on the death of his mother, regarded the princess with too much indifference to feel even hatred, though there were times when his flashing eye, as he saw the gross indelicacy of her manners, told what his tongue would never utter.

My duties as captain of the king's

guard took me often to the apartments of the queen mother, and the princess, whose appetite for admiration was excessive, condescended to play off all the artillery of her smiles and graces on an individual so humble as myself. But if I had really been, what she one day petulantly declared me, blind and deaf, I could not have been more insensible to her charms. The images of Adele and Aimée stood at the door of my heart, to guard it against the entrance of evil; and never, until they were forgotten, could a character like that of Margaret of France have seemed any thing but detestable to me.

For the first time since our boyhood there was restraint and formality between Henry of Navarre and myself, for neither of us dared speak of what was in our hearts; and the constant effort to avoid forbidden subjects made our interviews painful rather than pleasant.

Though mirth and feasting and merriment seemed to occupy the attention of every one about the court, from the queen mother down to her youngest page, I felt certain that we were standing on a volcano, whose uncapping might hurl us all to destruction; and from several slight indications, I could not doubt that the catastrophe was at hand.

Meanwhile Admiral Coligny, always calm and collected, seemed wholly unconscious of danger, and refusing to enter into the amusements of the court, spent his time in dictating to his secretary letters to the various Protestant princes and leaders, or in conversing with the young king, who visited him daily, and regarded him with equal respect and affection.

On the 17th of August, 1572, the wedding, deferred so long, at length took place. A platform had been erected before the great gate of the church of Notre Dame; and there, in the presence of a crowd of French and Navarrois nobility, Margaret gave her hand to Henry of Navarre. I was stationed near the platform during this inauspicious ceremony, and saw the glances of defiance and hate which deformed the beautiful face of the bride. When she was asked if she willingly took Henry of Navarre for her husband, she would not answer a word. Her brother Charles, who gave her away, whispered fiercely,

"Bow your head in assent;" but the proud head remained haughtily erect, and the face spoke scorn and determination.

"By the bones of my father, but you shall obey, proud minx," said the angry king in a low tone as he placed his hand on the back of her head, bending it forcibly down in token of assent. The Cardinal Bourbon, who performed the ceremony, understood the state of things, and affecting to be satisfied with this forced consent, the ceremony proceeded. At its close, Margaret retired into the body of the church with her family, to participate in the service of the mass, but Henry and the Protestant nobles of his train remained outside until the service was ended. At first the young bride did not hesitate to say to every one who approached her, that she hated the husband they had forced upon her; but his good-humored courtesy and forbearance evidently won upon her, and induced her to treat him with politeness, though of wifely duty and affection she made no pretence. Few females of her age could have resisted the attractions of Henry of Navarre, with all his graces of mind and person, and the reputation as a dauntless warrior and wise statesman which he had already acquired. But whatever heart the princess had to bestow, was already given to the young Count de Guiche; and she was alienated still more from her husband by her bigoted attachment to the church of Rome.

"I can see nothing in your religion," she said to me not long after her marriage, "but gloom and austerity. You can buy no indulgences, you can obtain no absolution; of what use are your priests only to show how hopeless your case is, without any possibility on their part of helping you? For me," she added, shrugging her shoulders, "I must have a religion that will give me peace of mind, if I am willing to pay for it."

In vain I attempted to make her understand that Protestants sought for pardon and peace alone from the Saviour of mankind, the only being who has power to dispense them.

"I see," she said, "you are not only a heretic, but a mystic as well, uttering the senseless babble of the schoolmen, which sounds strangely enough on the lips of a young nobleman, and a soldier to boot. Our French gentlemen have quite another method of entertaining young ladies, let me assure you."

"I am sorry my sentiments are not acceptable to your highness," I replied, "since it is out of my power to change them."

"Ah, barbarian," she exclaimed, playfully tapping me with her fan, "were it not that you came from the half-savage country of Navarre, I should despair of you entirely. But I trust we shall yet be able to civilize you in la belle France."

A bitter retort rose to my lips, but it

was repressed out of respect to the wife of my sovereign, and soon after I left the room. The next time I saw her, she was in her husband's court of Navarre, and it seemed to me that a lifetime of bitter memories and an ocean of blood rolled between us.

CHAPTER IX.

THE MASSACRE OF ST. BARTHOLOMEW.

THE newly married wife of Admiral Coligny did not accompany him to Paris, but remained on an estate near Angers, on the Loire, where she was beloved alike by Catholics and Protestants, for her active benevolence and the Christian virtues of her character. The admiral made frequent visits to his family and home, and on these occasions received repeated warning from various sources not to trust himself longer in the power of his enemies.

When leaving home for the last time, his fond wife urged him, by every argument she could employ, to relinquish the journey to Paris; but he believed duty called him back, and was completely deceived by the flattering attentions of the French monarch, though their very excess ought to have warned him of danger. At one time, after his last return to Paris, the king of France said to him, as he embraced him fondly,

"I have got you now, my good lord, and do not imagine I shall let you go again so easily."

"Have I not acted my part well, mother?" the same treacherous monarch inquired of Catharine after the departure of his victim.

"Yes, my son," was her reply, "you have done very well; but you must continue to play it for some time longer, until all is ready for the blow."

Lignerolle, a friend of the admiral, who was about to leave for the country, replied, when asked by Coligny to remain with him,

"No, my friend, they caress you too

much; it cannot all be real, and I had rather save myself with fools than perish with sages."

Had not the doomed Huguenots been fatally blinded, they could not have continued insensible to the premonitions of danger which surrounded them. The air was thick with portents of the coming storm. Low mutterings of distant thunder should have warned them that even now it was on the way. For myself, I had been certain, since the death of my queen, that evil was determined against the hated heretics, but loyalty to my king forbade the thought of flight.

My two dear friends, the Counts Montgomery and Rochefoucauld, had intended to leave Paris immediately after the marriage of Henry; but on various pretences they were detained by the king and his mother, who had formed their plan so as to include, if possible, all the leading Huguenots throughout the kingdom. The Duke of Montmorenci, wiser than his brethren, retired to Chantilly; and no entreaties could persuade him to trust himself near the court. Admiral Coligny was thoroughly weary of the levity and profligacy which reigned on every side, and which suited neither his years nor his deep religious convictions. He waited only till the close of the marriage festivities to ask leave to quit the capital, and at last obtained what he thought was a final audience. On his way from the Louvre to his lodgings, he was fired upon by an assassin hired by the Duke of Guise, and wounded in the left arm and the right hand, rendering the amputation of a finger necessary.

The young king of Navarre was deeply touched by the situation of his friend and almost father, and hastened to his bedside, accompanied by most of the Huguenot nobles of his suite. The demeanor of the noble old man was just what one would have expected from his character—firm, composed, and full of trust in God. In company with the Prince de Condé, son of the hero who fell at Jarnac, Henry went directly to the Louvre from the bedside of Coligny, and in the boldest and most indignant terms accused the king, in the presence of his mother, of being privy to the attempt on the life of the admiral, and declaring that neither himself nor his friends were safe in Paris, demanded immediate permission to depart.

Charles in reply expressed the most intense sorrow and detestation of the deed, declaring his resolution to inflict the severest punishment on its authors wherever they might be found. The queen mother acted her part perfectly, affirming with her usual duplicity, that if such a man as Coligny was thus assailed, neither herself, nor the king, nor the Duke of Anjou were safe. She assured Henry that the city should be searched, and no one permitted to leave it who could in any way be implicated in the crime. Charles went himself to wait upon the wounded hero, with every appearance of respect and affection; but he was never suffered to see him unattended by his mother, who took care that no private conversation should ever pass between them. She perhaps feared that the calm demeanor and noble forbearance of the old man under an injury so terrible, might shake the resolution of Charles, who felt as much veneration for Coligny as it was possible for his frivolous nature to entertain.

The extreme irritation of the French king, the instant search for the murderers, and the visit of the court to Coligny, with many minor indications of kind feeling towards the Huguenot party, served to quiet the apprehensions of Henry and Condé, who gave up the intention of immediately quitting Paris. Never was smiling treachery carried to a greater extent, never were victims more completely hoodwinked and befooled. In vain I told Henry my suspicions, in vain I urged him to draw off his friends in a body from the capital, carrying Coligny with us; the king replied gayly,

"Why, my good friend, you are in a very fever of suspicion and distrust. I do not believe implicitly all that is said to me here; but my new mother-in-law is not an ogress, nor my brother Charles a second Nero. Depend upon it, the devil is not as black as he is painted; besides, the admiral himself would never consent to steal away; he has entire confidence in the friendship of the king and queen mother."

Under pretence of apprehending another attempt on the life of Coligny, Charles set a guard over his house, and gathered all the Protestant nobility into the same quarter, saying they could in that way better defend themselves from any hostile movement on the part of the Duke of Guise. But the guard over Coligny's house was commanded by one of his bitter enemies, a quantity of arms were collected in the palace, and a large number of troops stationed in the neighborhood, while measures were taken to prevent any defensive weapons being conveyed into the Protestant quarter.

Thus the net was being drawn every moment more closely about us, while most were utterly unconscious of danger, though a few Huguenot gentlemen withdrew from the perilous position in which they had been placed, and retired either to the country or to a distant quarter of the city.

On Saturday, the 23d of August, Henry took his young bride to visit the admiral; and though Margaret soon returned to the Louvre, the king remained with his friend till evening, when he too went back to the palace. How little he imagined that during his absence the question had been discussed in council whether his life should be spared or taken in the approaching massacre.

"He is but a young bridegroom," said Catharine with a bitter smile; "it were a pity to make Margaret so soon a widow; and when his fangs are drawn by the death of his friends, his bite will be harmless."

It was finally decided to spare the Prince of Condé and the King of Navarre, but steps were taken to carry into immediate effect their sanguinary designs against all the other Huguenots in the capital. Badges were distributed by which the executioners might be known, and the signal agreed upon was the tolling of the great bell of the palace of justice, at midnight of St. Bartholomew's day, August 29th.

That terrible night stands out before my memory as distinctly as though its events occurred but yesterday. The air of the palace seemed tainted with the infection of the meditated crime. An ominous silence brooded over that quarter of the city surrounding the Louvre, in which the Huguenots were assembled as sheep for the slaughter, like that which precedes the bursting of the hurricane or an eruption of mount Vesuvius. All faces literally gathered blackness, for they seemed to grow dark with the vague terror and anxiety that pervaded every breast.

An attempt had been made by Catharine and Charles during the evening to avert suspicion by an excess of merriment; but even the craft and duplicity of the queen mother were unequal to this crisis. She would start and hesitate in the midst of a sentence, change color, and seem to listen anxiously; then she would recollect herself, and endeavor by a forced gayety to do away the impression made by her momentary forgetfulness. Charles, who was greatly attached to the Count Rochefoucauld, made a last attempt to save him by inviting him earnestly to remain and sleep at the Louvre. The invitation was declined, and the count left the palace to return no more.

CHAPTER X.

A NARROW ESCAPE.

When my friends had left the palace, I was so terribly oppressed, that, after posting the guards about the chamber of the king, in which nearly thirty Huguenot gentlemen had assembled to talk over the attack on the admiral and the position of affairs, instead of going as usual to my lodgings, I went to those of the admiral, intending to pass the night at his bedside. Short as the distance was, I saw many indications that something unusual was going forward. Individuals strangely attired were hastening stealthily through the streets, and when they met, stopped only to exchange a word or sign, and then glided away into the darkness, like ghosts revisiting the earth on some unhallowed errand.

I had reached the dwelling of Coligny, and was ascending the steps leading to his room, when suddenly the deep tones of the bell of St. Germain L'Auxerrois fell on my ears, and instantly the whole vicinity seemed transformed into a Pandemonium. The discharge of large and small arms, the shouts of savage fury, and screams of mortal terror, all were mingled in one unearthly sound, the like of which never saluted mortal ears. The Duke of Guise hastened to the house of the admiral, and was instantly admitted by the captain of the guard, who had every thing in readiness for the assassins. Six of the Swiss guards, stationed by Henry for the defence of his friend, were cut down while attempting to defend the passage against the ruffians, who made their way to the chamber of Coligny over their dead bodies. The old man was at prayer, perfectly aware of the fate that awaited him, and resigned to it. Rapid as the movements of the murderers were, I reached the chamber before them. I had armed myself, in addition to the sword and dagger, the only weapons the Huguenots were allowed to wear, with a sabre and pistols; and stationing myself near the door, succeeded in driving back a few of the assassins, but they pressed on in such numbers that I was speedily overpowered, and they rushed forward to the bedside of the hero, when one of them, holding his sword to the breast of the victim, inquired,

"Art thou the Admiral Coligny?"

"I am," he replied with perfect serenity. "Young man, thou should'st respect my grey hairs; nevertheless, thou canst abridge my life but little."

At this answer the ruffian plunged his dagger repeatedly into the heart of the admiral, while the others smote and stabbed him alternately. The Duke of Guise, who was stationed in the courtyard below, called out to inquire if the deed was done; and on being answered in the affirmative, ordered them to throw down the body through the window. When this was done, he spurned the bloody corpse with his foot, little thinking that his own senseless remains would be spurned in the same manner a few years later by the Duke of Anjou.

While this dreadful scene was going forward, I gradually recovered from the effects of the blow which prostrated me, and staggering to my feet, was about to enter the chamber, when a man enveloped in a large cloak came up to me, and seizing my arm, drew me through the corridor into the courtyard by a back passage which was quite deserted.

"You need not go further; your victory will be easy," I said to him, opening the collar of my coat.

He made no reply, but requesting me to mount a powerful horse which stood near, followed my example, and led the way through a labyrinth of lanes and alleys into an open street at some distance from the Louvre.

"Whither are you taking me?" I inquired at length. "I have no desire to escape; I only wish to die with my king and friends."

"Henry is in no danger," the unknown replied; "his life will be spared, but yours is not worth a moment's purchase if you go back to the Louvre."

"And why should I be spared, when all my brethren in arms are taken? If you are indeed desirous to do me a favor, give me my weapons, and suffer me to return and sell my life as dearly as possible."

"And have you then none to whom your life is of importance; no mother or sister who look to you as their only protector? Remember, the scenes of this night are to be acted over again in the provinces; and if report speaks truly, there are those at St. Florent who will need your protection."

These words recalled me to myself, for hitherto the blow I had received, and the loss of blood from a flesh wound in my arm, made me faint and bewildered.

"Whoever you are, whether mortal or angel," I exclaimed, "your words remind me of what I had nearly forgotten, that there are still duties which bind me to life, and I owe you more for recalling them at this moment than for the existence you have been the means of prolonging. But may I not know the name of my generous preserver?"

"It is of little consequence," replied

the unknown; "I have only repaid a debt owing to you since the battle of Clermont. Do you not remember saving a French officer from the hands of an infuriated rabble, who had sworn to put to death every Catholic prisoner? I am the man; so you see it is only a life for a life, and no great matter of gratitude."

By this time we had reached the forest of Fontainebleau, and here my companion turned to me, saying,

"I can go no further, for I shall be missed in the morning, and may besides do some good in the city. You can now make your way wherever duty or inclination call you. But stay; you must be unprepared for such a journey; here is a purse which may be of service to you."

Without waiting a reply, he turned his horse's head, and was out of sight in a moment, while, like one in a dream, I pursued my way towards the south.

Meantime, in the streets of the capital the work of death went steadily on. The tiger spirit of a Parisian mob was unchained, the streets were filled with armed executioners athirst for blood, the marked houses of the Protestants were forcibly entered, and the inhabitants dragged from their beds and murdered without resistance. Neither age nor sex was spared, and all the worst passions of depraved nature, let loose in the horrible anarchy, sated themselves with crimes too fearful to be told. The shouts and oaths of the murderers were mingled with the groans and cries of their vic tims, while above all the deep bells toll ed aloud, "More blood, more blood!" The gutters of Paris literally ran with the sanguinary current, drawn from the veins of the noblest and most virtuous men of France.

The scenes at the palace were, if possible, even more revolting than those of the streets. Charles IX., who with his mother and the Duke of Anjou waited in gloomy expectation in the halls of the Louvre, showed so many symptoms of wavering and indecision, that Catharine prevailed on him to hasten the concerted signal by ordering the bell of St. Germain to be sounded, instead of that of the Palace of Justice, as agreed upon. The party of royal assassins then proceeded to a balcony, from whence they could look out upon the streets, and while there the sound of a pistol was heard. The sound seemed to freeze the blood of the criminals, and Charles was about to issue an order to suspend the execution. But at that moment the tocsin sounded, flambeaux and lanterns flashed out from the windows of the papists, and the executioners, with the Duke of Guise at their head, began the work of death.

From that moment the fierce and sanguinary nature of Charles broke forth in all its frightful excess. He seized an arquebuss, and taking aim at the flying Huguenots, fired repeatedly, exclaiming as if mad, "Kill them, kill them!" to the butchers who filled the streets.

But where was Henry of Navarre while his dearest friends and faithful subjects were thus barbarously murdered? He had passed a sleepless night, and left his room in company with a few friends just before the break of day. In that wing of the palace the sounds of death were comparatively unheard; and though they were aware of some disturbance in the streets, they had no idea of its nature and extent. But almost immediately on leaving his room he was arrested with his relative the Prince de Condé, and brought unarmed before the blood-stained monarch, witnessing, as they passed on, the murder of some of their faithful friends and followers. Charles received them with a wrathful countenance, blasphemous lips, and with curses which froze the blood of the listeners commanded them to abjure their Protestant faith, or take the alternative. "Death, or the mass!" he exclaimed in the most violent manner; "death, or the mass!"

Henry answered briefly, but firmly, entreating the monarch to grant them life and liberty of conscience; but Condé firmly assured Charles that he would sooner die than do violence to his conscience.

"I am not so fond of life," he said, "as to peril honor and soul both to preserve it; and what I have seen this day has not served to recommend the Catholic faith to me."

In the first paroxysm of anger, Charles wished, notwithstanding the decision of the council, to add the two young princes to the number of his victims; but Catharine feared this extreme measure as impolitic, and prevailed upon him to grant them three days to consider, assuring them that, if at the end of that time they were not prepared to renounce their heretical opinions, they should be instantly put to death. They were then sent away under a strong escort, and Charles returned to his work of blood. The carnage continued all that day, and was renewed on Monday, and it was not until the third day that orders were given to stop the massacre.

The number of Huguenots who were slain on this occasion has been differently estimated, but I doubt not it exceeded seventy thousand. The inhuman orders of the king were but too faithfully obeyed in the provinces. The Rhone, Seine, and Loire ran with blood; carnage spread over all France, and crimes enough were committed in the space of a few weeks to blacken the history of a century. But in this midnight darkness I ought not to lose sight of the few illustrious examples of moral heroism and virtue which shine like stars amid the surrounding gloom.

The Catholic bishop of Lisieux contrived to save all the Protestants of that town. St. Heran, governor of Auvergne, replied to the king's letter in these noble words:

"Sire, I have received an order under your hand and seal, to put all the Protestants of this province to death. I respect your majesty too much not to believe that the letter is a forgery; and if, which God forbid, the order is genuine, I still respect your majesty too much to obey you."

The Viscount Orthey, lieutenant of

the king at Bayonne, answered in the following words:

"Sire, I have communicated the commands of your majesty to the inhabitants of the town and the soldiers of the garrison. I have found good citizens and brave soldiers in Bayonne, but not one executioner; on which account, both they and I humbly beg you to employ our arms and our lives in things we can effect. However perilous they may be, we will willingly spend therein the last drop of our blood."

Both these noble men died soon after having ventured to disobey the commands of the king, under circumstances which made it probable that they had perished by some of the means commonly used by Catharine de Medicis to rid herself of troublesome friends and dangerous enemies.

CHAPTER XI.

A DAY AT ST. FLORENT.

After my preserver left me, I continued my journey, faint, stunned, and bleeding, in a half-unconscious state, and must have kept a southerly direction almost by instinct, as I have no remembrance of the route. Some time during the day, on that terrible 24th, I arrived at St. Valerie, where an old and valued friend of my parents resided. How I reached the house I know not, for immediately afterwards all consciousness of pain and suffering was lost in insensibility. In this state I remained for many days, parched with fever, and unconscious of all that passed around me. Providence had kindly directed me to the house of a good Samaritan, and I wanted for nothing which the utmost care and kindness could bestow.

Two weeks passed away before I could continue my journey, and in that time what might not have happened! Life and death seemed hanging on my speed when I left Paris, and two weeks had fled, while I was lying helpless as infancy. It was with a sad and foreboding heart that I bade farewell to my kind friends, and pursued my solitary journey to Navarre. The horse provided by my unknown friend possessed a speed and strength I had never seen equalled, and bore me easily and rapidly forward, until the snow-capped summits of the Cevennes greeted my sight.

Passing through Montauban, I called at the house of Madame Toulan, but it was shut up, and she had removed no one knew whither. I could learn nothing of my family, only that there had been disturbances in the country, and terrible excesses had been committed by the Catholics wherever they were found in considerable numbers. This news was not encouraging; and though my heart refused to admit the possibility that any thing had happened to those beloved ones, still I rode forward with feverish speed, watching eagerly for every indication of civil strife in the country through which I passed.

Before noon of the second day I came in sight of the towers of St. Florent, and soon after rode up to the door of the lodge at the entrance of the grounds. To my surprise and dismay, the cottage was vacant and deserted, forsaken by its inmates and stripped of all its simple furniture. Shocked at the sight, I hurried forward, only to find the shrubbery about the chateau cut down, the flower-beds trampled under foot, and the trees in the avenue, those forest monarchs girdled and defaced by the ruthless hand of man.

Not a servant was visible about the dwelling, the court-yard was empty, the rooms dismantled and stripped of every thing movable, and the heavy articles of furniture so cut and defaced as to be utterly valueless. The picture-gallery had been visited, and the pictures were hanging in strips from their broken frames. The tapestry was torn from the walls of the state apartments; in a word, the destruction was complete.

Old as I am, I cannot recur to the unspeakable agony of that hour without tasting again the bitterness of the cup so suddenly presented to my lips. In my despair I called aloud on the names of my mother and Aimée. I ran from room to room, demanding some tidings of those dear ones from the senseless walls, whose lonely echo mocked my grief. At length I reentered my mother's room, a delightful apartment, with a southern exposure looking out on a terrace filled with flowers, and shaded by fruit-trees of various kinds. In the panelled walls was a secret closet, the favorite hiding-place of my sister and myself in childhood, and from whose recesses we were accustomed to receive good things when our behavior had given satisfaction.

Guided, as I believe, by the hand of God, I went to this closet with no distinct purpose, opening it in the restlessness of sorrow. The first object on which my eye rested was a note addressed to me in the well-known hand of Aimée. For an instant I gazed upon it, fearing that my senses deceived me; the next, I seized it eagerly, and in the delirium of joy pressed it to my lips, bedewing it with tears. As soon as I regained command over my feelings, I opened the note and read the following words:

"I am writing this note to you, my beloved Henri, because I hope and believe that, if you are spared to return to our desolated home, you will not fail to visit this dear hiding-place of our infancy; and thus you will learn that our God has mercifully preserved us from the wrath of our enemies. If you will go to old Ambrose, the miller at the castle of Pau, he will give you sure tidings of us, and direct you to our place of refuge. I dare not tell you in this, lest by some chance it should fall into the hands of the wretches who are about to visit us for the second time since you left St. Florent. But I must close, for we have only a few moments left for escape. Adieu. May the blessing of our Father above ever rest upon you, my own dear brother."

After thanking God from the depths of a grateful heart, I turned away with renewed strength and courage from the desecrated home of my boyhood, for since they were safe who had made it home to my heart, I could give up every thing else without a murmur.

At the further end of the bridge which connects the castle of Pau with the hamlet lying on the other side of the stream, is, or rather was, a mill, which supplied the inhabitants of the castle, and was called the mill of Jane d'Albret. Old Ambrose Pinel was the miller, a stanch Huguenot, and one of the best of men. A large apartment above the mill had been the scene of various interesting meetings between the early reformers and different illustrious individuals of Europe. There Marguerite of Savoy, the beloved sister of Francis I., and a firm patroness of the Reformation, held a conference with Calvin, Peter Martyn, and Erasmus, who came from Geneva for that purpose.

To this spot I hastened in search of Ambrose, and to my great joy found him at home, though just about to start on a long journey through the southern part of France on important business. Had I been one day later, all hope of seeing my mother and sister would have vanished, at least for many weeks. It was one of those events in my life, and they have been many, in which the hand of an almighty Friend was distinctly visible, directing my path, and ordering events which were utterly beyond my control. My children, I believe in a special providence, so special that it takes cognizance of those minute details which go to make up the sum total of human happiness or misery. From my soul I pity the materialist who sees in all that occurs only the result of blind chance; and the equally wretched Christian, who believes that his Father is too far beyond and above him to take note of his every-day cares and trials. Surely He who numbers the hairs of our head, and watches over the sparrow in its search for daily food, must be interested in all that concerns the welfare of his children, and nothing but unbelief can deprive us of the infinite blessedness of such a care. But I am digressing.

Ambrose Pinel received me with surprise and joy unbounded, for the details of the massacre had reached him, and he believed me among the victims.

"Your friends," he said, "mourn for you as among the dead, and this last blow has crushed them to the earth. How great will be their joy and gratitude to find you given back to them, as it were, from the grave."

"But where am I to find them, good Ambrose? Every moment is an age until we meet."

"They are hidden in one of the wildest gorges of the Cevennes," he replied, "in the house of a forester who is true as steel to his friends and his faith. I will myself guide you to the spot, for I have intrusted the secret to no one. My motto is, 'If you would make sure of the safety of a secret, keep it to yourself;' and I have always found it work well."

We were soon on the way, and as we journeyed, I related to the good man all the events of that fearful night in Paris, so far as they were then known to me. He looked upon my escape as miraculous, and was inclined to believe my preserver an angelic messenger sent by God for that special purpose.

I was too anxious and too weak to

combat the proposition, and we pressed forward, unmindful in the excitement of the hour of the symptoms of fatigue exhibited by the noble animal which had borne me so far and so well. All night we made our way through the wild and desolate passes of the Cevennes, and in the morning came in sight of the cabin of Pierre, in which those dearest to me had found shelter.

That meeting I shall not attempt to describe. There are moments in life to which words are utterly incapable of doing justice, and this was one of them. When the first transports had subsided, so that we could look in each other's faces, I was shocked to see the change in that dear countenance which had made the sunshine of my life from infancy to the present hour. It was very pale and thin, and the smile it had formerly worn was now seldom visible; still the spirit's peace shone through it, lighting it up with a radiance indescribably beautiful.

"I am not ill, my dear son," she said in answer to my look of anxiety; "I have not been even seriously indisposed through all this fearful time; but we suffered much at the chateau; and then the horrible news from Paris must have crushed me, but for the supporting hand of God. But you are spared, my own dear Henri. I am permitted to see your face once more, and all other causes of sorrow seem as nothing."

"Ah, Henri, brother, can there be in all the world such happiness as ours?" exclaimed Aimée, her blue eyes sparkling through tears, and her sweet face eloquent with emotion. The months that had passed since my departure from home had changed my sister from a lovely and loving child to a devoted, high-souled woman. She seemed to have no thought for herself, but in her watchful care of others, was constantly developing some new and beautiful trait of character, whose existence we had never suspected. Heretofore I had loved her as a charming pet; now I learned to revere her as far superior to myself in all the higher qualities of human nature.

"How is this, dearest?" I inquired; "you are talking of happiness, when I find you driven from home, stripped of every thing, and dependent for shelter on the hospitality of a peasant. From whence comes the happiness of which you speak?"

"From the mercy of God, who has spared to me my mother and brother," she replied with a fond smile; "and having them, I seem to possess all things. This hut is a home with those I love, and St. Florent would be a desert without them. But, dear Henri, we know nothing of your history; we have only the blessed consciousness that you are with us. Now we wish to know how it has all happened."

I then told the story, and as I ended, Aimée exclaimed,

"If that unknown preserver was not an angel in disguise, I would willingly travel on foot to Paris to find him and express my gratitude. I will ask God every day to permit me some time to know and thank him."

"I trust your prayers will be answered, dearest," I replied, "for I would gladly do something to render my debt of gratitude less oppressive. But you forget that I too am ignorant of all that has happened at St. Florent, and must know every thing, painful as it is to think you have suffered while I was away, unable to comfort or assist you."

"The fact of your absence, my son, so

far from being an aggravation of our sorrows, was a blessing, for which we were devoutly thankful, little dreaming that you were in still greater danger in that terrible city. Had you been with us, your young life would have been thrown away in vain; for what could you have done against a band of infuriated ruffians, led on by men who have grown old in wars? Rather let us bless God, who in his own way hath preserved us from our peculiar perils, and given us this blessed meeting, in a time of universal terror and distress. But the recital of the past is too painful for me voluntarily to go over it, though Aimée will relate to you all you wish to know. At your happy age, sorrow does not make an impression so deep as to render it painful to look back upon it. On the contrary, the joys of to-day are rather enhanced by a remembrance of the sufferings of yesterday."

CHAPTER XII.

AIMÉE'S STORY.

"If I am to make the recital," said Aimée, "I shall commence by telling you, dear Henri, how much we all admired and loved your charming Adele. I was every day finding some new beauty or grace in her, and I could never have imagined that one so young could be so wise and good."

"How long was she with you at St. Florent?"

"She stayed nearly a year, then her grandfather took her away, and continued absent some months, after which they came back for a short time; but when we had learned to feel her necessary to our happiness, they left us for some distant province, where M. Fauchet has many friends.

"For some weeks after their departure we were very quiet, though rumors of war filled the air on every side.

"But one day last spring our good butler Antoine had been at Pau, and heard somewhere on the road that bands of Catholics were organizing in Bearn and Navarre, for the purpose of sacking the castles of the nobility and inflicting every possible injury on the Huguenots. We were alarmed, of course, but for two days heard nothing more of the marauders, and trusted we were to escape. But just at sunset on the third day, I saw through the window an armed troop coming up the avenue, led by Victor Bourdon, whom you may remember as the son of the Catholic advocate in Montauban. He left his men stationed round the house, and entering alone, told us with great civility that it was necessary for him to search the house for a heretic who was supposed to be concealed there. In vain we assured him M. Fauchet had been gone for months; he was polite but determined, and the search was made. He accompanied the men himself, carefully restrained them from insult and plunder, though the contents of the wine-cellar and larder were at their disposal.

"For several days he remained at St. Florent, as he said, for the purpose of protecting us from injury, and then departed, leaving us more frightened than hurt, though very thankful for our deliverance."

"Victor Bourdon, do you say? I little thought in Montauban that I should ever owe him so much. I hope some time to meet him, that I may prove my sense of obligation for his kindness and forbearance."

"It is hardly right, my son," said my mother, "to permit you to lie under the weight of an imaginary obligation. M. Bourdon was undoubtedly lenient in his treatment of us, but the reward he proposed to himself, and seemed fully to expect, was nothing less than the heart and hand of my precious child."

"What!" I exclaimed. "How dared he, the minion of a tyrant like Charles, the leader of a band of ruffians and murderers, to raise his eyes to a noble Protestant maiden? Such effrontery does indeed cancel all sense of obligation."

"Nay, Henri," said Aimée, laughing gaily, though her cheeks would have shamed the blush rose, "you take it too seriously. M. Bourdon probably thought himself condescending greatly, in the flush of his new honors, to stoop to an obscure country maiden, and a Huguenot to boot. He would not understand you if you were to speak of presumption on his part. But we will not talk of him on this happy day. If he deceived himself when he came to the chateau, he certainly could not have done so when he went away."

"But you have said nothing of the final scene of destruction. Tell me how you managed to escape from the wretches who have laid our dear home in ruins."

"I can tell you but little of that terrible day, Henri; it seems to me like a confused and fearful dream. Reports from Paris had reached us which were so dreadful as to be wholly incredible, for it did not seem possible that a being in the form of woman could be so cruel and wicked as Queen Catharine. There were disturbances all around us, and the servants of the chateau had been for days almost paralyzed with fear. Still our dear mother was calm, for she trusted in

God; and besides, we were so lonely and defenceless, that our very weakness seemed to guarantee us from harm. But we learned our mistake only too soon. Good Ambrose Pinel, the miller at Pau, came to St. Florent early on the morning of Sept. 2d, and gathering all the servants together, begged my mother to dismiss them at once, that they might seek safety elsewhere. The plate, and such other valuables as could be collected, were hastily secreted in the garden, our jewelry and the money in the house disposed of about our persons, and then with our faithful Claudine, who refused to leave us, we took a last lingering look at the pleasant and beloved home to which we were bound by so many fond recollections, and were ready to follow our friend and guide.

"'I shall take you,' he said, 'by a secret and subterranean passage, known only to myself and one other since the death of the Sieur de Beauvilliers. So much time has already been spent, that Soulier and his band are undoubtedly near the chateau, expecting an easy victory. But God knows how to deliver his children. The secret passage will bring us out beyond their outposts, and we can then make our way to a hiding-place in the Cevennes, where you will find safety if not comfort.'

"While he was speaking, the sound of a trumpet and the tramp of horses was heard, and looking out, we saw the chateau surrounded by a savage band, with a fierce-looking warrior at their head, whose very face seemed to freeze my blood. The servants had fled, and the chateau was firmly secured, so we had sufficient time, before our enemies could effect an entrance, to escape from the house. But before leaving I wrote a hurried note to you, my brother; and recollecting our childish fondness for the secret closet, placed it there, feeling sure that when you returned to St. Florent and found us absent, that would be the first place to which your steps would be turned."

"It was so, sweet sister; and I owe you more for this thoughtful kindness than words can express. Until I received it my heart seemed to stand still with terror; but your precious note was like life from the dead. But what progress did you make in the subterranean passage? I remember hearing my father speak of it in my childhood, but had forgotten its existence until now."

"We made our way slowly and with difficulty. In some parts the passage was high and wide enough to permit us to walk easily, but in other places the stones and loose earth had filled up the way, so that we were obliged to creep on our hands and knees. At length we came out into an opening or cave, in which we rested for a while, and then for the first time we learned from Ambrose the circumstances which had led him to our rescue. One of the band had been in the habit of visiting the female servant at the mill, and knowing her to be a good Catholic, ventured to intrust her with the secret of their intended attack on St. Florent and other places in the vicinity. Andrea, though a bigoted papist, felt kindly towards us, and believing that her master could in some way avert the threatened evil, went to him with the tidings. Ambrose immediately formed his plans and hastened to the chateau, where he arrived, as I have told you, just in time to save the whole household from death, or a fate worse than death

"When he had finished his recital, we moved forward again, and passing up a steep and narrow stairway cut in the rock, soon found ourselves in the open air in the forest of Bondy near the ruined chapel of La Fere. From thence a path, beaten by the shepherds and their flocks, leads to the heart of the Cevennes, and travelling all night, we reached this hospitable dwelling the following day. Pierre is a friend of Ambrose, and received us joyfully, and here we found what was of the first importance to us—rest and safety. Our dear mother was completely exhausted with fatigue and care, and for several days after our arrival here could not leave her bed.

"Then came that terrible time of which I can never think without a shudder, when the news of the massacre of Paris reached us through Pierre, and we believed you, my brother, among the victims. I will not cloud this happy day of reunion by dwelling on our agony. It seems to me that you have been restored to us by angelic agency; for if your preserver were a mortal like ourselves, he was surely sent by God to save a life so precious to many."

I remained at the cottage of Pierre a week to recruit the strength which my journey had exhausted, intending then to join the Huguenot forces which were assembling at various points under leaders who had escaped the general destruction. But what was to become of my mother and Aimée? St. Florent was now in ruins; the chateau a mere shell, having been revisited and fired by the ruffians since I saw it on my way to Pau.

While we were debating this point, a messenger came to us from the widow of Admiral Coligny, begging my mother to come to her at her chateau near Angers on the Loire, where she had fixed her permanent residence.

"I am sad and lonely," she wrote, "and as the valued relatives of my martyred husband my heart clings to you, and nothing could now make me so happy as your society. We are a community of Protestants, and the few Catholics in the neighborhood are under the spiritual direction of a truly good and tolerant bishop, so that we have hitherto escaped the horrors which have convulsed the other provinces of unhappy France. Do not wait to write, but come to me at once with the messenger who takes this. He is shrewd and faithful, and will guide you safely to Auvergne."

This letter removed every obstacle from our path. It provided a safe and honorable asylum for those dearest to me, and left me free to devote myself to the cause which, hallowed by the blood of so many martyrs, seemed more sacred and precious than ever before. We left the abode of the kind peasant with many thanks and such recompense as our means would allow, and made our way towards Angers. It was a most charming country in which Madame Coligny had chosen her abode, and the chateau seemed the home of order, comfort, and peace.

In this pleasant retreat, and under the care of one who would love and cherish them as they deserved, I left my friends and retraced my steps towards Nerac, hoping to obtain some intelligence from the King of Navarre. But nothing had been heard from him since his fatal marriage, and I employed myself in collecting my scattered troops and enlisting others, that when the day for action should come we might not be wholly unprepared.

CHAPTER XIII.

OLD FRIENDS UNDER NEW CIRCUMSTANCES.

Henry of Navarre and his young relative the Duke de Condé were detained in Paris as state prisoners for many months after the massacre of St. Bartholomew. The thrill of horror which pervaded all Europe on hearing of that dreadful crime, warned Charles and his mother that they might go too far; and though the heretic husband of Margaret was an object of fear and hatred to them both, they judged it best to dissimulate, and wait a more favorable time for the carrying out of their plans. But though the young lion had been caught in the toils, he was far from being a safe or quiet captive. No arguments or threats could win from him one word of concession in regard to his faith, and he made no attempt to conceal the horror with which he regarded the queen mother and her son as the murderers of his best and dearest friends.

From time to time we found means to communicate with him through a trusty messenger; and when every thing was in readiness for his return, he contrived, with the tact and ready wit which distinguished him above most other men, to make his escape from Paris with Condé and a small retinue of faithful followers. Every step of the way was full of dangers, but a power higher than that of man guided him through them all, and with a joy too deep for noisy demonstrations we welcomed our prince and leader to the camp near Nerac, where a few thousand veteran troops awaited his orders. As he rode through the long lines, and marked the upturned faces full of a devotion which knew no bounds, his own countenance glowed with enthusiasm, and turning to Condé, who was at his side, he exclaimed,

"To-day I rejoice that I am a Bourbon, privileged by blood and birth to command such men as these."

Then turning towards the troops, who had been formed into a hollow square, he addressed them in the following words:

"Men, brethren, and fathers, I went away from you last year a careless, happy boy: I come back to you now an earnest, determined man, ready to do and dare all that can be done or borne in defence of the sacred cause of civil and religious liberty. By the precious blood which flowed like water in the streets of Paris, by the memory of that martyred mother whom we all revered and loved, I solemnly vow never to sheathe this sword until I and my brethren are free to worship God according to the dictates of our own conscience. If your leader is youthful, he is at least deeply in earnest; and if older generals may excel him in ability, you shall see that he knows as well as they how to die for his country and his faith. If in the battle you follow the white plume of Henry of Navarre, I promise you it shall always be found in the path of honor and glory."

This address, delivered with all the fire and ardor of his nature, was received with loud bursts of enthusiastic applause. As the voice of one man came up the shout from the army,

"We will live or die with our leader and king, Henry of Navarre. We swear it."

From motives of policy, rather than

affection, Henry resolved on demanding his bride at the hands of her mother and brother, who had hitherto refused to give her up. After a time, however, the crafty Florentine thought it advisable to have a spy in the camp of the enemy, and Margaret was sent, greatly against her will, with a numerous train of high-born beauties, to play the part of queen in her husband's court of Navarre.

Those who remembered the noble and virtuous Jane D'Albret, whose simple dignity marked her born to command, while her kindness made her the mother of her subjects, sighed as they looked on the painted and gilded puppet who occupied her place. Destitute of the semblance of principle, Margaret disdained to throw over her profligacy even the thin veil of conventional propriety; and the daily and nightly orgies of the French portion of the court disgusted the Huguenots to such a degree, that most of them left the court, while Henry, disguising as far as possible the indignation excited by his wife's unblushing vices, made active preparations for taking the field.

For more than two years our little army was constantly on the move in various parts of France, meeting the enemy in skirmishes and engagements with various results, sometimes gaining an important advantage, then sustaining a disastrous defeat, and always preserved from destruction by means little less than miraculous.

At the battle of Coutras, where, by the military skill and dauntless bravery of Henry, a threatened defeat was turned into a glorious victory, we first taught the French monarch that the Huguenots were a foe not to be despised; and from that time the young king of Navarre took his place among the princes of Europe as an object of love and pride to the friends of the new faith, and of fear and dread to its enemies.

Towards the close of the battle, as I was leading on a corps of reserves, I received a sabre wound in my right side and shoulder, which rendered me insensible. After what seemed to me a long sleep, during which I had a multitude of harassing dreams, I awoke one afternoon wondering greatly where I was and what had happened to me. I attempted to raise my head, and found to my surprise that it was no longer under the control of my will, but remained a lifeless weight upon the pillow. The right arm was equally immovable; but after repeated attempts, I succeeded in drawing apart the curtains of serge which surrounded the low pallet on which I lay.

I saw a neat and comfortable room, belonging, it would seem, to the better sort of farm-houses which are so common in Bretagne, simply furnished, and lighted by two small windows with diamond-shaped panes, over which shades of dark paper had been placed to exclude the light. On a bench by the fire sat an old woman busily engaged in preparing something over the coals, and croning to herself an ancient provençal ditty. As I dropped the curtain from inability to hold it, I heard the door open and some one enter, who inquired of the nurse in a low tone,

"Is there any change in your patient?"

That voice thrilled through every nerve of my body, and it seemed to me would have had power to recall my soul from the very gates of death, for it was the voice of my friend and tutor M. Fauchet. An involuntary exclamation brought him to my bedside with surprise and pleasure speaking through every feature of his well-known countenance.

"Ah, Henri," he exclaimed, "my dear, dear young friend, God has heard our prayers, and given you back a second time to us from the very grave. Blessed be his holy name."

I attempted to speak, but my tongue was strangely stiff, and I could only murmur,

"What is it? Where am I?"

"You are in the house of a good and true man near Coutras, and have lain here in a state of unconsciousness for weeks. You were badly wounded at the battle of Coutras, and a violent fever was the consequence. The king, who loves you, and has mourned over your danger, sent his own physician to attend you, and to his skill, I think, under God, you owe your life."

"And you?" I inquired, unable to say more.

"I was on my way to England," he replied, "and learning that some of the sufferers had been brought here, I stopped to inquire into their situation. When I saw you, my pupil, my own dear son, think you I could have gone forward, leaving you perhaps to die? But I am disobeying the commands of the leech in talking to you at all. You must now take a composing draught, and sleep again, and to-morrow I will see you, and answer all your questions as far as I am able."

Too weak to question or contend, I obeyed his orders, and soon sank into a dreamless sleep. The next morning I awoke faint and feeble indeed, but free from fever and with a calm and collected brain, and full consciousness of all that was passing around me. I had not long to wait for M. Fauchet. When he entered the room, I saw with pain the ravages which time and sorrow had made in his face and form. His once erect figure was bent, his face pale and thin, and he walked slowly, like one oppressed with years or care. He greeted me with all the affection of former years, but to my first question,

"Where is Adele?"

He replied with a hesitation I never before saw in him,

"My child has been for some time past with an old and trusted friend in Auvergne; but we are now on our way to England, where Madame Toulan has gone, and offers us a home for the little time that may still remain to me in the flesh."

"Is Adele then in this house?" I eagerly inquired, forgetting all besides in my interest in that fact.

"She is here," he answered slowly; "but why should it concern you, my son?"

"Why does it concern me? How can you ask me such a question? It concerns me because she is my adopted sister—next to my mother and Aimée, the dearest thing on earth to me; because we have been separated for years, and my heart yearns to see her once more. Why should you seek to keep us asunder? Have you less confidence in us now, than when we were comparative children?"

In my eagerness I had forgotten pain and debility, but M. Fauchet said with a smile as he rose to leave the room,

"Your cheeks are flushed, Henri, and your whole frame agitated; calm yourself, I entreat you, and to-morrow you shall see Adele."

That was a long, long day, but the morrow came at length, and with it an increase of strength, which, to those ignorant of the power of mind over matter, must have seemed marvellous indeed. Every time the door opened to admit the old Breton nurse, my heart beat almost audibly; and when at length M. Fauchet appeared, followed by his grandchild, my agitation deprived me at first of the power of utterance.

It was the Adele of Montauban, the very same; and yet how changed! Time had not stolen away one lovely trait; it had only heightened and perfected them. There was the same union of simplicity and dignity, of childlike sweetness with womanly maturity, of ingenuous frankness and maidenly reserve. I am sure my soul must have spoken through my eyes as I gazed upon her, though at first my tongue was utterly powerless. By degrees however, as she sat by my side, and in her own charming way went over the past and related her own story since we met, my senses came back to me, and we were once more the Henri and Adele of other years.

"I little thought in those days," she said playfully, "that my brother Henri would become the famous Huguenot soldier and wise leader which report speaks him, though my heart predicted a brilliant career for you. How glad and proud it has made me in my solitude to hear of you as the trusted friend of your king, and the brave commander of men fighting for the noblest of all causes, religious liberty."

Could any thing be sweeter or more welcome than such praise from such lips? I listened like one entranced, but M. Fauchet said gravely,

"Do not forget, my child, that our good Henri is still in the flesh, and praise, however pleasant to human nature, is still dangerous."

"Forgive me, my father," she replied with a blush which heightened every charm, "but I have not often of late been tempted to forgetfulness by any wish to go over the happy past. Monsieur Beauvilliers on this sick-bed is to me only the Henri of Montauban, in whose presence I was always accustomed to think aloud."

"From my soul I thank you, dear Adele, for your favorable opinion; but it will never render me vain, while I know myself to be so far below the ideal we both formed in our youth, and which is constantly before me as an incentive to exertion."

"I am glad you do not consider yourself quite perfect," she said with an arch smile, "for in that case I should soon lose sight of you entirely. But we have overstaid the time allowed us by the nurse, and shall be held accountable if your symptoms are worse after this visit."

In vain I assured her that her presence was the best medicine in the world for me, that I felt myself every moment growing stronger. M. Fauchet was firm, and hurried her away, leaving the room, as it seemed to me, in total darkness.

I saw her twice again, but those interviews I shall not attempt to describe. As I look back upon them from this distance, they seem to have less of earth in them than heaven; for though our hearts ran together like drops of water mingled into one, no word of love escaped my lips. Adele was to me country and religion impersonated; and in the delicious languor of convalescence it was inexpressibly sweet to lie and watch her graceful movements, to hear her burning words, and to feel her devotion stealing into my heart, filling it with the determination to live or die for the sacred cause of liberty.

M. Fauchet had delayed his departure on my account; but when I became able to sit up and walk with the aid of a staff, he felt it necessary to join Madame Toulan, who was impatient at his long delay. There was no leave-taking between Adele and myself; in my weakness I could not have borne it. We parted as usual with a simple "good-night," and the next morning before I awoke she was far away, leaving only a sweet and precious memory to console me for her loss.

CHAPTER XIV.

A PLEASANT SURPRISE.

A FEW days after the departure of M. Fauchet and Adele, my nurse entered the room, and in her Breton dialect attempted to cheer my loneliness, but her homely proverbs fell on unheeding ears until she exclaimed,

"After all, there 's nothing so bad but it might be worse. Now in the other part of the house there 's a poor young officer worse off than you are, and not a soul but his servant who ever saw him before."

"A sick officer! And why have I never heard of this until now?"

"Because you had enough to do to think of yourself, and because the young lady, God bless her sweet face, said you were not to hear of it until you were much better; and I trow she 's one of those who can lead people by a silk thread just where she pleases."

"But who is this wounded officer; and what is his name?"

"He was on our side in the battle, so they say, and he is a born gentleman, that is easy enough to see; but as to his name, I never heard it."

"Is he getting better, so that he can see me? If so, I think I could, with your help, manage to reach his room."

"I have no care of him, but I will ask his servant, who watches him day and night, and bring you word, though you 're not fit yourself to be visiting the sick, and you a mere shadow."

Word was soon brought that the sick man would see me on the morrow, and I spent several hours of the intervening time in trying to imagine which of the officers of our army it could be who was thus sharing my sufferings and inactivity. Most of the Huguenot leaders were known to me, for our common cause and common perils had bound us closely to each other. After wearying myself with this fruitless endeavor, I wisely resolved to dismiss the subject until the next day, certain that whoever he might be, every thing had been done for him that care and skill could accomplish.

The next morning, leaning on a staff and the arm of my nurse, I proceeded through the large kitchen floored with brick, to the apartment of the wounded officer on the opposite side of the house. He was sitting in a large chair supported by pillows, and the pale, worn face was wholly unknown to me. But as I approached, the first words he spoke in answer to my greeting startled me to such a degree that I had hardly strength to seat myself in the chair by his side. It was the very same voice which had spoken to me on the night of the twenty-fourth in Paris; I should have known it among ten thousand. The stranger saw my agitation, and said with a smile,

"Am I then an object so frightful as to alarm a brave man like the Sieur Beauvilliers?"

"Do not speak of it," I replied vehemently; "you know well the cause of my emotion. You know when and where we met before; but how is it that I find you here, my friend, my preserver?" and as I held his hand, I am not ashamed to own that my tears fell freely over it.

"You know me, then?" he said, struggling to conceal the emotion which nearly overcame him; "I should not have believed it possible, under the circumstances of that horrible night, that my voice alone would be so long remembered."

"The most minute details of that night are burned into my soul," I replied, "and can never be effaced; how then could I fail to recognize my generous protector, the man to whom I owe more than life, the power of protecting those dearest to me? But why do I find you here, suffering in the cause of the persecuted Huguenots?"

"You find me here because the crimes of an infamous king and queen mother have opened my eyes to the abominations of the accursed system which has helped to make them what they are; because I could not draw a free breath in that den of robbers and murderers called the French court.

"When I left you that night, I went back to Paris, not to assist in the work of death, but if possible to save some of the unfortunates whose cries pierced my heart. But when I found the streets filled with incarnate demons thirsting for blood, and urged on by the anointed assassins at the Louvre, I turned and fled, feeling as though the earth must open and swallow up the actors in that fearful tragedy.

"My father the Count de Viomenil, recently dead, possessed a chateau near Rheims, and to that place I directed my steps. An aged aunt inhabited the chateau, and had long been known as a friend and protector of the Huguenots, whose faith she was suspected of sharing, though such was the benevolence and purity of her life, that by all the country people she was regarded as a saint. To her I opened my heart with all its doubts and misgivings, and her sympathy and wise counsels were like balm to my troubled spirit. She placed the word of God in my hands, and though at first I read it in deference to her wishes, I soon became interested in it as a message from God to my guilty, darkened soul. I will not dwell on that time; it is sufficient to say, I left Rheims determined to seek Charles to acquaint him with the change in my belief, and then either renounce the military profession and retire to my estates, or join my brethren who were fighting under Henry and Condé."

"But how dared you," I inquired, "thus to beard the lion in his den? The risk was fearful."

"For myself I had no fear," he replied with a calm smile. "I have never valued life so highly as to hesitate about risking it when any thing valuable was at stake. Besides, strange as it may seem to you, I loved Charles not as the monarch, but the man, and my affection was returned by him. We were playfellows in childhood, and whatever might be his treatment of others, to me he was uniformly kind. It was a painful and dangerous task to tell him that my services were no longer at his command—that my allegiance was to be withdrawn and sworn to another; but it must be done."

"Did you indeed seek Charles of Valois with such a purpose, and yet live to tell the story?"

"Listen, and you shall hear. I hastened to Paris and to the Louvre, but found the king confined to his couch with a disease which baffled the utmost skill of the physicians. The unhappy man was racked with intense pain, and covered with a bloody sweat which seldom left him. 'Blood, blood; it is all around me,' was his continual cry; it seemed as though the righteous retribution of God had already commenced, and was slowly consuming its victim. He was evidently dying, but my presence seemed to give him satisfaction, and he begged me to stay by him to the last. I could not leave him, guilty as he was, for he seemed forsaken of God and man; but I obtained from him a written permission, when all was over, to retire to my estates in Guienne, assuring him that since the 24th of August I could never again fight under the banner of the Duke of Guise.

"The day before his death the king lay in an insensible state, and fearing treachery from Henry of Anjou if I awaited his accession, I left Paris secretly, and made my way at once to the Huguenot camp. Concealing myself under the name of my mother's family, I have fought as a private, and made my way up to my present position unknown to all save my faithful valet and friend Etienne, who at the battle of Coutras bore me insensible from the field, and brought me here, where his care and skill have nursed me back to life again."

"Did you know the name of your fellow-sufferer?" I inquired.

"Yes; M. Fauchet, who visited me often, once mentioned you incidentally, and I made inquiries which satisfied me who you were. I have waited impatiently, I assure you, for this hour."

I stayed with him until increasing fatigue warned us both that we were far from strong, and then went back to my room, thankful to God who had thus unexpectedly raised me up a friend in my solitude. After this we met every day, and each succeeding interview only cemented more closely the bond of friendship which united our hearts.

For myself, I gained strength hourly, and Etienne declared with a broad smile that Monsieur Beauvilliers had done his master more good than all the medicines given him by the leech. As my wound, though doing well, would not for many weeks admit of my going into active service, I resolved to visit my mother and sister at the hospitable abode of Madame Coligny, and invited M. Viomenil to accompany me. After some hesitation, he accepted the invitation gladly, and we began at once to prepare for the journey, which we intended making on horseback, and which would occupy nearly three days. My servant had been wounded at Coutras, and was now in Navarre; but the valet of M. Viomenil was a host in himself. He was quick-witted, active, and faithful, and possessed an infinite variety of resources, so that we wanted for no comfort which his skill could procure.

It was a lovely afternoon in autumn when we first caught sight of the beautiful Loire, shining like a belt of silver beneath our feet, while in the distance the blue mountains of Auvergne, with their rocky summits rising like gigantic barriers, seemed to guard the lovely valley beneath. The town of Angers, built in the form of a crescent, occupies the slope of a hill, and descends down to the very margin of the river. Its streets are steep, narrow, and dark, and we rode through them as rapidly as possible, on our way to the chateau, which was situated on the left bank of the Loire, at the distance of a league from Angers.

As we entered the grounds of the chateau, the deep verdure and refreshing shade were so grateful, that we lingered in the avenue, admiring every thing about us, when suddenly the sound of voices fell upon our ears; then light footsteps were heard, and soon, emerging from a side path, I saw my sister Aimée, her cheeks glowing, her eyes shining like stars, and her straw hat thrown back, come flying towards me.

"It is my brother, my Henri," she exclaimed as she threw her arms about my neck, for I had dismounted on seeing her approach. "Oh, thank God that you are able to come to us once more." In her joy at seeing me, she had not noticed that any one was with me; but now, as she saw my companion gazing upon her, she blushed, drew back, and whispered, "I thought you were alone."

"I am not alone, dear sister," I replied; "but you will not regard my friend as a stranger, when I tell you he is M. Viomenil, my preserver on the night of St. Bartholomew, in Paris."

"Is it possible!" she exclaimed, her whole face bright as a sunbeam. "Then heaven has heard my prayers in permitting us to know and thank him. Oh, sir," she said, giving him her hand, "if you could see my heart, you would know how fervently I thank you for saving a life so precious to us and to all who know him."

"I am already rewarded a thousand-fold for a simple act of humanity, mademoiselle," he said, bowing over the hand she had extended; "but your thanks are very precious, and I accept them with joy and pride."

"How delighted mamma will be," said Aimée. "I hardly know which of you will receive the warmest welcome, we have so longed to know the preserver of our Henri; but let us hasten to the house, that mamma and Madame Coligny may partake the happiness."

In a few moments we reached the house, and were received by my beloved mother and her friend with a welcome which even now warms my heart as I recall it. To M. Viomenil the chateau of Angers was a new world. He had never known mother or sisters, and his knowledge of female character had been chiefly acquired at the French court. To him therefore the dignity and intelligence of Madame Coligny, the matronly grace and sweetness of my mother, and the sparkling loveliness of Aimée, had all the charm of novelty; while his heart owned for the first time the power of female excellence and virtue. A few weeks after our arrival at the chateau he came to me, saying,

"My good friend, you brought me to this house well knowing what it contained, and how impossible it would be for me to associate with your lovely sister without yielding my heart to her attractions. You cannot therefore be wholly unprepared for what I have to tell you. I love Aimée Beauvilliers, not with a light or transient passion, but as man should love the partner of his being for time and eternity. Have I your permission, as her guardian and protector, to tell her this? And if I am so happy as to gain her consent and that of your mother, will you, my friend, trust me with the charge of her happiness?"

Nothing could have given me greater pleasure than this declaration, and I frankly told him so. I knew him to be honorable and high-minded naturally; and no one could associate with him, as I had for many weeks, without feeling the influence of his genuine piety. "You have not only my full consent," I said to him, "but my best wishes for your success. Aimée's love will be a rich treasure; but I am sure you deserve and will appreciate it as you ought."

The suit of M. Viomenil was successful; and when, with renewed health and vigor, we left Angers to join Henry at Nerac, we were not only brothers in arms and in heart, but joined by a dearer, sweeter tie, the love of our precious Aimée. My mother could not consent to part with her child immediately; but in one year M. Viomenil was to claim his bride, and until that time both my mother and sister would remain at Angers under the powerful protection of Madame Coligny.

CHAPTER XV.

MY VISIT TO ENGLAND, AND ITS CONSEQUENCES.

Henry of Navarre and Margaret of France had parted, after dragging on a miserable existence together for two or three years, during which time the conduct of Margaret became constantly more shameless and abandoned.

In compliance with the wish of the king, I attached myself to his suite, and was constantly with him in court or camp. Aimée had become the Countess Viomenil, and had gone with my mother to reside on an estate of the count's in Guienne; so I was quite alone, and was often employed by Henry on various missions to the different courts of Europe. At length matters of state rendered it necessary that an ambassador should be sent to England, to counteract, if possible, the influence which Henry III. was supposed to be exerting over Queen Elizabeth. I was selected for this purpose; and after a hurried visit to Guienne, where I found my sister the happiest of the happy, I embarked at Calais and landed at Dover, from whence I went immediately to London. To me, all England held but two persons, my tutor and Adele, and I found myself scanning every strange face I saw, in the vague hope that those dear countenances might by some chance bless my sight; but I could learn nothing of them. There were many French *emigres* in London and its environs, but no one knew aught of M. Fauchet.

The week after my arrival I had an audience at Whitehall, and there for the first time saw England's Elizabeth, the hope and stay of the Protestant cause throughout Europe. The audience chamber was a grand and imposing apartment, the assembly splendid beyond description; but amid it all I had eyes only for the queen, whose look and air, and indeed her every gesture, proclaimed the brave and undaunted spirit of her race. She received me graciously, saying, in the hearing of all her courtiers,

"So highly do I prize the friendship of my brother Henry of Navarre, that I would gladly do him a pleasure even by the sacrifice of my own interests; and I rejoice to know from the lips of his friend and ambassador, that hitherto God hath preserved him from his enemies, and given him assurance of ultimate success."

She then presented me to her principal nobility, and placed me under the charge of Lord Hunsdon, her chief lord in waiting and her maternal uncle; with the direction that nothing should be wanting to make my stay in England as agreeable as possible.

There was so much ceremony and etiquette in the court of Elizabeth, that I found it rather tedious, until the young Lord Essex, with soldierly frankness, offered me his friendship, declaring he admired so much the bravery of the Huguenots that, next to his own sovereign, he would rather serve under Henry of Navarre than any other monarch of Europe. With this gifted but unfortunate nobleman I spent many happy hours, and to him I owe the happiest hour of my life, that in which I found again the companion of my youth and the friend of riper years, my own dear Adele.

We had been riding into the country at some little distance from London, when, passing a low house almost buried in shrubbery, Lord Essex remarked,

"Two years ago that house, which now looks so desolate, was full of life and cheerfulness, and Lady Essex and her mother loved better to visit there than at any other house about London; and now I think of it, Beauvilliers, they were countrywomen of your own who lived there, an elderly lady, an old man, and a beautiful young girl, now all gone."

"What was the name?" I inquired, my heart beating almost to suffocation.

"The name of the old lady I have forgotten, but that of the young girl was Adele Briancourt. I have remembered it because both my wife and myself admired her so much."

"Did you say they were gone? Do you know where they went?"

"You know them then, since you manifest an interest so deep in their movements. Well, I can tell you but little, and that little, I fear, far from satisfactory. The old grandfather died first, then the aunt took a fever and followed him, leaving the young girl alone, but for a servant, old Madeleine, who had come with them from France."

Poor Adele, how my heart ached for her in her loneliness and sorrow, and how ardently I longed to shelter her in that heart from all the storms of life; for I had learned within the last few moments that Adele Briancourt was dearer to me than any other being on earth.

"Can you tell me where Mademoiselle Briancourt is to be found?" I inquired in a tone of forced calmness, though my whole soul was convulsed with emotion.

"I am sorry to say, I do not know," he replied; "for though Lady Essex entreated her to come to us after the death of her aunt, she declined with many thanks, and I heard afterwards accepted a situation as French governess in the country; but where, we have never been able to discover."

"The secret shall not baffle me long," was my inward resolution as I parted with Lord Essex at Whitehall, and retired at once to my own lodgings. I arranged my affairs, and obtained leave of absence for a fortnight; then taking my faithful valet with me, I left London with the determination of finding Adele before seeing it again. I had formed no definite plan of proceeding; it seemed to me that my heart would guide me to Adele; and every morning I rose with renewed strength and courage, only to retire at evening weary and almost disheartened. There were many families who had French governesses, but none of them resembled the image stamped on my memory; none of them was the grandchild of M. Fauchet.

At length, when the fortnight had

nearly expired, and I must either neglect my duty or return to London, a violent storm came on without warning, drenching me to the skin, exposed as I was on horseback, with no adequate protection. At that moment my servant pointed out a dwelling at hand, in which we might hope for shelter and hospitality.

It was a long low building, irregularly constructed, with a view to comfort rather than beauty, and surrounded with extensive pleasure-grounds, laid out with equal taste and skill. A carriage-drive bordered with noble trees led up to the house, and the park was stocked with deer, who turned to look at us as we rode through the avenue, then darted away through the forest glades with the swiftness of thought. Why do I dwell on these details? Because every thing connected with that spot is of interest to me; because, as I look back, every minute detail comes up before me with the vividness of a picture on which I gazed but yesterday.

We rode round to the courtyard at the rear of the house, and dismounting, gave our horses to a servant who came out and invited us to enter. I requested the privilege of going into the kitchen to dry my wet garments; but as I entered, what was my astonishment to hear the exclamation in my own language,

"It is Monsieur Henri!" and as I looked hastily up, I saw before me the well-known features of Madame Toulan's Montauban servant, Madeleine.

"Where is your young mistress?" was my first inquiry; "where is Ma'amselle Adele?"

"Not far away, you may be sure, when you see my good Madeleine," said a sweet voice at my side; and turning, Adele Briancourt stood before me, a little thinner and paler than when I saw her last, but otherwise unchanged. Time and sorrow seemed to have no power over her spiritual beauty; in loneliness and dependence she was the same cheerful, happy being, shedding the sunshine of her own heart over all around her.

"We are fortunately alone," she said, when the first joyous greetings were over, "as the family are all absent to-day at a fair in the next town. They are good and worthy people; but I am selfish enough to wish to have you all to myself for one day, before sharing your visit with others."

"Ah, dear Adele," I replied, "I have sought you sorrowing for many days, and when I was ready to despair, God has given you to me; my heart is too full of happiness to care for aught else."

"I heard of you in England, my friend, and there were times when my heart almost broke with longing to see you once more; but pride forbade the obscure governess to make herself known to the courted, flattered ambassador."

My answer to this remark I shall not attempt to give. It is enough to say that we were very happy; and as my time was short, I had made such good use of it, that before the return of the family at evening, I had won the consent of Adele to go back to France with me, never more to be separated on earth.

The next day I returned to London with a glad heart, to finish my business there, and to make preparations for claiming the lovely and beloved companion who was to share my return to our native country. To my great surprise, on my first audience Queen Elizabeth condescended to interest herself in my little story, which she had heard from Essex, and complimented me on what she was pleased to term the reward of constancy. She graciously expressed a wish to see the lady of my choice; and accordingly, when I brought Adele to London as my wife, she was presented to the queen, and though perhaps I ought not to say it, not one among the beautiful women who surrounded their sovereign outshone my charming bride.

On our return to France, our first visit was to Guienne, that the new daughter and sister might be welcomed there as she deserved. At the urgent request of my mother and sister, I left her with them during the campaigns which ended with the glorious battle of Ivry; after which I took her to a chateau I had purchased near Angers, where several happy years were spent, until the accession of Henry IV. to the throne of France; after which we removed in his train to Paris.

CHAPTER XVI.

THE ACCESSION AND DEATH OF HENRY IV.

Henry III. of France, who ascended the throne after the death of Charles IX., had been at school and college with the king of Navarre, and was inclined to look upon him with more favor than any other member of his family had ever been. Catharine de Medicis was dead, gone to her last account with all her innumerable sins upon her head; and thus Henry was saved from the domestic influence ever at hand to lead the unhappy Charles into public and private crimes. But the reign of Henry was far from being peaceful or happy.

The Duke of Mayenne, a powerful nobleman, formed a league of all the discontented spirits in the realm, and took possession of the capital, driving out the king and court. Henry III. then formed an alliance with Henry of Navarre, and together they laid siege to Paris. While in camp there, Henry was assassinated by an agent of the League, brought for that purpose from the monastery of Troyes. He lived a few days, and then expired, leaving his crown to the king of Navarre, if he had strength and skill sufficient to seize and retain it.

Paris was in a state of open rebellion against its legitimate sovereign. Many of the large towns were held by a small minority of turbulent nobles; the small towns were either wavering or disaffected, and the rural districts presented every shade of opinion within a few leagues. One province was nearly all Catholic, another all Protestant, and still another equally divided. All respect for the law had long since disappeared, for the vices of the court had banished all notions of morality. In fact the whole fabric of French society was disorganized, and no common principle of action was strong enough to bind together the members of any great party.

Immediately after the death of the king of France, Henry of Navarre entered the room, and declared that by the laws of the realm and the will of the late king, he, as his lawful successor, assumed the crown. A few of those present saluted him and shouted, "Vive Henri Quatre!" but many stood aloof, unwilling to commit themselves at that moment to any course of action.

Just then the Duke of Longueville, at the head of a large body of nobles, entered, and coming up to the new king, in a long oration pointed out to him the dangers of his situation, and besought him to embrace at once the Catholic religion as the only means of securing the nobility on his side. I was standing by the king, and saw the strong effort made by him to control his indignation while the duke was speaking. He was very pale, but perfectly calm as he replied in burning words which are indelibly impressed on my memory.

"Among the many wonders, gentlemen, with which God has been pleased to visit us during the last twenty-four hours, that which is caused by your proceeding is what I should least have expected. Your tears, are they already dried? The memory of your loss and the entreaties of your king, not three hours dead, have they so soon vanished? It is impossible that all here can have agreed on all points of what I have just heard uttered, to take me by the throat at the first moment of my accession, at so dangerous a moment to think to drag me to that which men have been unable to force so many humble persons to do, because they knew how to dic. And from whom can you expect such a change of faith, except from a man who has none at all? Would it be more agreeable to you to have a king who is an atheist? And in the day of battle, would you follow with confidence the will and guidance of a perjured apostate? Yes, it is as you say, the King of Navarre has suffered great disasters without being shaken by them. Can he cast off spirit and strength on the steps of the throne? However, that you may not call my firmness obstinacy, nor my prudence cowardice, I reply to you that I appeal from the judgment of this company to yourselves, when you have had time to think, and when there are more peers of France and officers of the crown present than I see here on this occasion. Those who cannot wait for riper deliberation, and who yield to the brief and vain success of the enemies of the state, have my full leave to seek their wages under insolent masters; I shall yet have all those among the Catholics who love France and their honor."

This address, poured out with the impetuosity of his fiery nature, carried conviction to all hearts, and as soon as it was ended, the brave Givry came in, and throwing himself at the feet of the king, exclaimed,

"I have just seen the flower of your brave nobility, sire, who reserve, till they have taken vengeance, their tears for their dead king, and wait with impatience for the commands of their living monarch. You are the king of the brave, sire, and none but cowards will abandon you."

But though the nominal king of France, the sovereignty existed for years but in name. Henry was constantly in camp, reducing strong fortresses held by partisans of the League, and endeavoring, as far as possible, to arrange measures of finance, in order to replenish the exhausted treasury. His bravery, generosity, and the wise statesmanship that distinguished all his movements, produced their natural effects, and won to his cause thousands who at first hated and opposed him. In a few years after his accession he entered Paris in triumph, not only as a conqueror, but as the acknowledged and venerated father of his subjects. He had contended with the arms and intrigues of the whole Catholic world, and foiled them all; he had overcome the hatred of his people, vanquished his enemies, subdued his rebellious subjects, and turned coldness, indifference, and even prejudice into love, reverence, and admiration

I confess, as I looked upon him in the Louvre, the centre of a brilliant throng of the highest nobility of France, the first gentleman, as he was the first monarch of Europe, and remembered his childish words in the garden of Pau, I felt proud of him as a countryman, a friend, and a sovereign, under whom one might gladly live, and for whom one might willingly die. He was now in the zenith of his power and fame, and had just obtained a divorce from Margaret of Valois, which left him free to contract any marriage which inclination or state policy might dictate. The proudest houses in Europe would gladly have opened to receive his addresses. The choice fell upon Mary de Medicis, a member of the same Florentine family whose alliance had already been so disastrous to France. If the new queen ot Henry IV. had less craft and cunning than her kinswoman, she proved to be equally unscrupulous and destitute of principle. During a long life she never made one faithful friend, and died at last in a garret in Cologne, the wife and mother of kings, dependent on the charity of a domestic for the daily bread which sustained her miserable existence.

The office conferred upon me by the king, that of superintendent of finance, rendered it necessary for me to reside in Paris; and as the Count de Viomenil, now commandant of the king's guards, also took a house in the capital, we were all very happy in our reunion. My mother found her youth renewed in the children of her beloved Aimée and Adele, while the young and still lovely mothers were among the brightest ornaments of the court.

But a terrible reverse awaited us. In the midst of power, prosperity, and splendor, the monarch was cut down by the blow of an assassin, and died instantly, leaving his son and heir, a mere child, under the regency of Mary de Medicis, a bigoted Catholic, and whose hatred of the Huguenots equalled that of Catharine.

The dauphin, afterwards Louis XIII., was a proud, sullen, and cruel boy, so destitute of natural affection even in early childhood, that Henry IV. replied to his mother, when she expostulated with him for correcting the child,

"Madame, you may well pray God to preserve the life of your husband, for I foresee that you will suffer from the violence of your son when you have no other protector."

The words were prophetic.

The queen regent, anxious only for her own supremacy, and devoted to the indulgence of her own vices, committed the royal boy to the care of ignorant and wicked persons, seldom allowing the friends of his father even to see and converse with him. Her own manner towards him was utterly destitute of affection, cold and repelling to the last degree. Thus he grew up, a singular compound of opposing bad qualities. Proud, yet timid; weak and vacillating, yet treacherous and revengeful; moody and reserved, yet incapable of keeping a secret: such was the son of the bravest, frankest, and most joyous being who ever swayed the sceptre of France.

It soon became evident that under the regency of Mary no favor would be extended to the Huguenots, who were deprived of all places of honor and emolument, and made to feel in various ways that their day of court favor had gone by. To the count and myself this was a matter of very little consequence, for we had only tolerated Paris from affection for the king, and retired to our estates, glad to escape from a life we had never loved, to the domestic felicity which awaited us there.

Several happy years passed away in obscurity while you, my children, were growing up in health and beauty; and every year bound my beloved wife more closely to my heart, as the various excellences of her character were unfolded in the every-day intercourse of life. But humble and inoffensive as we were, our enemies had not forgotten us. Numerous warnings were sent us from time to time that evil was determined against us, so that we were induced to make investments, so far as we could do so safely and quietly, in England, preparatory to our removal to that country.

At length the storm burst; and though the edict of Nantes, by which universal toleration was secured throughout France, was not formally repealed until many years later, the Huguenots were everywhere hunted and persecuted like wild beasts.

Through the mercy of God our families were enabled to make their escape in time, and reached England in safety. Among the beautiful shades of Richmond we found two houses, side by side, where for twenty years we have enjoyed a degree of peace and prosperity which seldom falls to the lot of mortals.

Elizabeth of England preceded our own beloved sovereign to the grave, and James I. was now seated on the throne, a weak; timid, pedantic prince, whose very virtues partook so largely of absurdity as to render him an object of ridicule to his subjects. But he was a kind friend to the Huguenot emigrants, and was wise enough to perceive that the thrift and mechanical skill of France was being emptied into the lap of England by this process of expatriation.

And now, my children, my pleasant task is ended, for I need not recall scenes with which you are even more familiar than myself. You know how I loved your excellent mother, how deeply I mourned her loss; but you cannot know the joy with which I look forward to a reunion with her in that blessed land, of which the Lord God and the Lamb are the light, and where they go no more out for ever.

www.ingramcontent.com/pod-product-compliance
Lightning Source LLC
LaVergne TN
LVHW011218110826
845150LV00006B/1460

* 9 7 8 1 4 2 5 5 1 6 4 4 4 *